Christmas Presence

Mira Publishing House CIC.
PO BOX 312
Leeds LS16 0FN
West Yorkshire
England
www.MiraPublishing.com

Christmas *Presence*
By Daniel M Warloch
ISBN: 978-1-908509-03-1
First published in Great Britain 2012 by Mira Publishing House CIC.

Printed and bound by www.beamreachuk.co.uk

A full CIP record for this book is available from the British Library.
A full CIP record for this book is available from the Library of
Congress.

Mira Intelligent Read

Acknowledgements

Special thanks go to my family for their kind words of encouragement during the course of writing this novel, and also Mira Publishing for having the belief in me.

I would also like to mention Isobel Jones, a former pupil of Hoole Church of England Primary School whose short story was the winner in a competition I arranged, along with the help of the teaching staff, in the Spring of 2011. Isobel's prize was to be one of the main characters in Christmas *Presence*.

I must acknowledge Jacky Newcomb and Alicen Geddes-Ward for their comprehensive study of the magical world of faeries in their faerie book, *"A Faerie Treasury"* (Hay House Publishers), which aided me in the writing of this novel.

Hardly anyone see faeries (or fairies), full face and in bright light. Most people see them slightly out of straight-on vision, or out of the corner of an eye. When you look at them, they vanish. Many people see small faeries as little balls of light or shadow, flitting around the room. These lights can be white or pastel, usually.

I hope you all get the chance to see one one day ...it will change your view of life and the world forever ...

Twelfth Night, the fifth of January, is when all Christmas decorations should be removed so as not to bring bad luck upon the home.

Long ago it was thought that leaving the decorations up would cause a disaster. People believed that Tree-Spirits lived in the greenery that they decorated their Christmas tree and house with.

The greenery was brought into the house to provide a safe haven for the Tree-Spirits during harsh midwinter days.

Once this period was over it was necessary to put the greenery back outside to release the Tree-Spirits into the countryside once again.

It was thought that if you left the greenery in the house, the Tree-Spirits would cause untold mischief and. . ?

"Hi ...

I've been wondering how long it would be before you came around to reading my book.

But what made you decide?

Was it the hairs on the back of your neck standing up when you first picked it up, or the tingle on your fingertips?

"Anyway, let's not concern ourselves with that at the moment, what matters is that you have taken your first step in my incredible and terrifying journey.

"Before you begin, I would strongly suggest that you make yourself as comfortable as possible, as you may not want to put the book down once you have started. But more importantly, if you decide to rest your eyes, please ensure you keep the book well hidden because you wouldn't want the wicked, awesome ...

"Sssh, please don't say a word; remain calm and just act normally. I have an awful feeling someone is watching us. Can you sense it as well . . ?

" ... Not to worry, it's fine; don't be alarmed or worried. It was only my imagination running riot as usual ... or was it. . ?

"I'm so sorry about that. I hope I haven't put you off reading the rest of my story.

"Now where was I ... Oh yes, I remember now.

"To tell you the truth, I've had a hard time of it lately, owing to the fact that I have to hastily move at short notice from one deserted hideout to another. I'm also finding it extremely difficult concentrating due to the lack of sleep, and more worryingly, I've completely lost track of time. And to add to my misery, the freezing cold draught coming in through the shattered window over to my right is making it difficult for me to put the

v

words down onto paper. I am just hoping and praying that someone finds the time and patience to translate my wobbly handwriting ...

"Sorry. How rude of me. I haven't introduced myself properly, have I?

"My name is Barnaby Tinker-Tailor, and I believe it's only right that I tell someone about my unearthly experiences that began on the evening of the 23 December 1967. I was just twelve years old at the time, and if I'd known then what I know now, I most certainly would have done things a whole lot differently ..."

Christmas Presence

By Daniel M Warloch

© 2012

Chapter One

23 December 1967

"Are you sitting comfortably? Then I'll begin..."

Looking back to my early childhood I can always remember being happy and contented, living with my Mum and Dad in our cosy semi-detached house on the fringes of the Yorkshire Moors. But, unfortunately for me, that wasn't to last for long, as you will soon find out.

I was an only child; that meant I was spoilt like mad. Definitely no complaints on that front, thank you very much.

Mum worked part-time at the local woollen mill, and Dad was employed as a long-distance lorry driver with a haulage company based on the outskirts of Leeds. Sadly, this meant he was away from home for days at a time, sometimes weeks. Yet he always made a special effort to be home with his family over the Christmas period, and especially to be home in plenty of time to organise the decorating of the front room with our tacky Christmas decorations ...

Dad was making an almighty racket, rummaging around in our dusty loft. Mum was busying herself in the kitchen, singing along to the Beatles Christmas number one that was playing on the radio and I was rolling around in fits of laughter on the floor in the front room, watching Laurel and Hardy on our black-and-white television making another fine mess of decorating someone's living room. (It would be a number of years before colour televisions were readily available).

Eventually, Dad came down from the loft, coughing and spluttering, covered from head to toe in dust and cobwebs. Securely nestled under one arm was our trusty cardboard box full of Christmas decorations, and wedged under the other was our tired looking Christmas tree we'd had since before I was born.

"Dad, do we have to put these old worn-out decorations on the tree? Can't we go out and buy some new ones? And I thought you said we were going to have a real tree this year!"

By this time I was on my hands and knees, sifting through the various outdated decorations. The thick layer of dust that had coated them over the previous twelve months constantly irritated my nose, causing me to sneeze a number of times.

"I tell you what, Barnaby, I'll make a deal with you," said Dad, attempting to unravel the Christmas tree lights from around his clumsy fingers. "If you buy two or three decorations with your pocket money, I'll go out and buy a real tree in the morning. What do you say to that? Is it a deal or what?"

"Deal, Dad. And my mates at school mentioned to me the other day that there was a Christmas fair in town, so there's bound to be a few stalls selling fancy Christmas decorations. Can we go there after you've bought the tree?"

"You'd better go and ask your Mum. She's in the kitchen making the mince pies, and from the high-pitched wailing that's coming from in there, sounding as though she's trying to strangle next door's cat," said Dad, chuckling away to himself as he continued unravelling the lights.

I was now becoming bored sifting through the worn-out decorations. So, except for the ones I'd made at school when I was in Pre-School, the rest I tossed back in the box.

"You're not thinking of putting those three on the tree again this year are you, Barnaby?" inquired Dad with a hint of a smile. By this time he was now cautiously laying the disentangled lights across the back of the couch.

"Yes. Why not? I can't see anything wrong with them," I snapped back, carefully brushing away the dust from said decorations with one of my neatly pressed handkerchiefs.

Before I could say another word, Dad had headed off towards the kitchen, mumbling something unintelligible under his breath.

The three decorations in question were a plasticine character I'd named Knuckledown, and two well-loved dolls Mum used to play with when she was a little girl. Mum had named the dolls Rosie Apple and Tickety-Boo. I decided to keep the names for Mum's benefit; also, I couldn't be bothered trying to come up with alternative ones.

Knuckledown's head and body were carefully shaped from various colours of plasticine, and his arms and legs were made from a combination of pipe cleaners and toothpicks which I'd painstakingly glued together. Perched on top of his deformed head was a battered felt cowboy hat with a bird's feather tucked down the side of the hatband. I found the hat in the attic. I presumed it was from one of Dad's old toys.

You may be interested to know that the feather came from an exceptionally large black crow I found injured under a pile of dead leaves in the back garden. And because of all the noise it was making I decided to call it Rustle. At first I thought it might have been a seagull coated in oil, due to its remarkable size.

I kept the bird well hidden inside a shoebox in the shed we had at the bottom of the garden, and I fed it daily with warm milky bread until it was strong enough to fly away. After a great deal of time and effort I eventually managed to nurse it back to health. That was six months ago. I became quite attached to Rustle, yet I knew one day I would have to let him go. It seems a lifetime ago now. I do miss him.

As for the two dolls, well I didn't go overboard dressing these two up. (I am a boy after all, not a sissy.) I attached a pair of hand-made paper wings to Rosie Apple, along with a dazzling fairy wand my cousin Isobel gave me. As for Tickety-Boo, I carefully fashioned an assortment of coloured crêpe paper into a dress fit for a princess, along with a matching pair of wings I'd made from a lace handkerchief Mum gave me. And clipped to her long flowing yellow hair was a glamorous sparkly crown made from a cut-down Cornflakes box.

I can well imagine you're probably sitting there wondering why on earth I called the odd shaped plasticine character Knuckledown, so I'll tell you. I named him after our games teacher Mr. Harris who had a striking resemblance to Knuckledown. Old man Harris used to always bawl and shout at me during games lessons for me to 'knuckle down' and get a move on. I hated games!

Chapter Two

24 December 1967 AM

"Come on Barnaby, get a move on, we'll be setting off for the fair once your Dad gets home with the tree," called out Mum from the kitchen, the intoxicating aroma of bacon and eggs drifting up the stairs.

The first thing I spy when I peek out from under my bedclothes is my four-foot 1966 World Cup Final poster pinned onto my bedroom wall, along with an assortment of Dr Who and Thunderbird stickers. As you might guess, the World Cup poster takes pride of place. Wow! What a final that was. It will be something I will remember for the rest of my miserable life ...

"Get a move on, lazy-bones. We won't wait all day for you, and don't let me have to remind you again," shouted Mum from the foot of the stairs.

"It's blooming well freezing in my bedroom. It's like sleeping in the outside toilet," I called back, cold breath escaping through my chattering teeth. "And when are we going to get that fancy central heating in *our* house? Most of my mates at school have got it. You should feel the warmth when you walk into their bedrooms." As usual, Mum didn't reply to my demands.

I then began to go through my morning ritual of counting to ten, leaping out of bed and running around the room like a crack-pot trying to keep myself warm while getting dressed.

On reaching ten, I quickly threw off my blankets and leaped out of bed, wincing as my sweaty feet touched the cold linoleum.

"And w-why can't we have blooming fitted c-carpets as w-well?" I stammered from the chill in the air, whilst hopping around the room on one foot, struggling to pull on my socks.

Some ten cold minutes later I was dressed and seated downstairs by the kitchen table, tucking into an unappetising fried breakfast.

"If you'd come down when I called you the first time, your breakfast wouldn't be cold," Mum pointed out to me.

"Not to worry, Mum, I like cold bacon and eggs. What time are we setting off for the fair?"

"When your Dad eventually gets back from the shop with the Christmas tree; and like everything else with your Dad, he always leaves things to the very last minute. So don't be surprised or upset if he comes back empty-handed," answered Mum as she carried on washing the dishes from breakfast.

As I was mopping up the leftover eggy bits from around the edge of my plate with my bread, Dad suddenly appeared in the kitchen doorway, dragging in what looked to me like a humungous Christmas tree.

"You'll never get that through the kitchen and into the front room, it's huge. And just look at your shoes, George, you're trailing dirt all over the kitchen floor." As Mum was scalding Dad, I couldn't help but noticing her trying to stop herself from laughing.

Once we'd all calmed down, we began to move the kitchen furniture to one side to give Dad sufficient space to manoeuvre the tree into the front room.

Fifteen sweaty minutes later, with Dad constantly cursing under his breath and Mum snapping back at him for using foul language, we eventually managed to navigate the tree into the front room in one piece, and surprisingly, without scratching any of the furniture.

"It's one of those new fandangle Scandinavian trees that take ages to shed its needles," Dad proudly informed us, at the same time carefully pulling out the hundreds of pine needles embedded in his sweater. And also, may I add, looking slightly embarrassed from his remark.

"I think you've been sold a dud, Dad. I can see at least a million needles covering most of the carpet, and hundreds that've ended up on the furniture from where you've dragged the tree in from the kitchen."

Aware of what I'd just said we all burst out in fits of laughter, which luckily eased the tension between Mum and Dad.

"I think you may be right there, son. Come on, let's head off to the fair; we can sort the tree out when we get back," giggled Dad, wiping away the tears with the back of his hand, at the same time continuing to pick the needles from his sweater.

Chapter Three

Finally, we set off to the fair. But only after Mum had insisted we sweep up the hundreds of pine needles from the carpet and brush away the ones that had landed all over the living room furniture.

After dumping the carrier bag full of pine needles in the dustbin, the three of us excitedly made our way down the road to the bus stop. Luckily, we didn't have to wait too long in the freezing, blustery wind for the bus to arrive.

Some fifteen minutes later the bus pulled up by the main entrance to the fair. Stepping down onto the pavement we were greeted by the rich soothing voices of carol singers, combined with the characteristic sounds of rattling tambourines coming from the Salvation Army Band positioned a few feet from the bus stop. And, as I'd expected, the fair was jam-packed with hundreds of bad tempered people, all pushing and colliding with one another, doing their last-minute Christmas shopping.

"Mum, can I go and wander around the fair by myself for a short while? And then meet up back here next to the hot dog stand, PLEASE? And I promise I won't get lost," I pleaded, my puppy-dog eyes staring up at her.

She smiled down at me before answering, "Go on then; but you have to promise me that you won't go wandering off outside of the fair, and more importantly, don't talk to any strangers, apart from the stallholders I mean."

"I won't Mum, and thanks. I'll see you back here in thirty minutes." I didn't bother waiting for a response, and

I was out of her sight in a matter of seconds.

Thrusting my cold hands deep into the pockets of my coat, I began to check out the dozens of stalls, shivering and taking in the curious sights. I was also listening to the dazzling sounds coming from all sides, all mixed with the beautiful bouquet of toffee apples, brandy snap, doughnuts and hot dogs that drifted around in the cold morning air.

"If I have any pocket money left over after buying the Christmas tree decorations," I thought, my mouth watering from the aroma, "I'll treat myself to a hot dog with onions, all smothered in tomato ketchup – yummy, yummy!"

As I was being constantly elbowed in the face, and jostled from side to side by my elders, I spotted an unusual-looking brightly-coloured stand positioned at the far end of a long line of stalls. And for some unknown reason, there didn't seem to be any sign of activity around it. It looked as though everyone in the vicinity was trying to avoid it, or they weren't even aware of its existence in the first place.

"That's weird," I remembered thinking at the time, as I made my way toward the stall, butterflies in the pit of my stomach.

"Good morning young man; is there anything I can tempt you with today?" came the raspy voice of the old man who was seated directly behind the stall.

I hastily backed away after my initial sight of him. He was wearing a long brown cloak that covered his shoulders with the hood high up around his face. Yet on closer inspection, he did have a warm friendly smile which made me relax a little. He reminded me of a monk I'd seen on a recent religious TV programme. Also, I couldn't help but noticing him rubbing his wrinkly hands as he peered

9

across at me. I took a few more tentative steps back from the stall, expecting at any second to bump into some of the other shoppers around me. But my immediate area was totally deserted of foot traffic.

"That's odd," I muttered, my breath pluming before me in the crisp, cold morning air. Then in the blink of an eye, it felt as though someone had turned the sound off. There was no chatter or laughter close by, or any kind of noise in the distance for that matter. In addition, there was no hysterical screaming drifting over from the children on the roller coaster that was positioned at the far end of the fair. Nothing. It seemed as though I'd suddenly gone deaf. Thankfully I hadn't, as I could hear the old man gibbering away to himself. Yet for some strange reason, I wasn't too concerned about the lack of sound, because it felt so peaceful and tranquil!

"Nutty or what?"

"Is there anything in particular you're looking for today? I know what will interest a boy of your age. What about these two Tree-Spirits? I can certainly guarantee that they will keep away any nasty spriggans or bogles whilst they're safely in your house over the Christmas period," he informed me, revealing from beneath the table an antique-looking wooden box with ornate patterns carved into its sides.

Stretching his lean body over the stall, he gingerly handed the box over to me. Without thinking, I carefully reached across and took it from him. As my cold fingers brushed the top of the box, the lid flew up without my having to lift it, and to my pleasant surprise, the box contained two unusual-looking dolls, both delicately

10

wrapped in a fine white lace.

"Interesting," he muttered under his breath.

"Pardon."

"Nothing," he replied, eyeing me closely and rubbing his chin.

"Please handle the Tree-Spirits with utmost care. You wouldn't want to wake them up and frighten them, now would you?" he said, looking somewhat sheepish as though he was hiding something from me.

I hadn't realised, but I'd lifted one of the dolls out of the box, and I was in the process of inspecting it in my trembling fingers. And you know what? I could have sworn it had stirred a little in my sweaty hands. With that spooky thought in mind, I carefully placed it back in the box, re-covering it with the lace, before carefully resting it on an assortment of strange-looking Christmas cards and brightly coloured wrapping paper. I'm not chicken to admit it, my heart was beating like a drum in my chest from the weird sensation of holding the unusual doll, and it took me a few minutes to get my breathing back to normal.

"I'm sorry mister, I don't think I could afford these two fine dolls. Do you have anything for ten shillings? That's all I have to spend," I asked, nervously chewing away at my bottom lip.

For some unexplained reason I couldn't pull my eyes away from the mysterious-looking box, and the hairs on the back of my neck began to prickle and rise. And apart from the stillness in the air, I couldn't help but sense that the people milling around were totally ignoring me. As far as they were concerned, I didn't exist.

"I tell you what. It seems likely that you may be the only customer I'll have today, so I will let you have the

Tree-Spirits for ten shillings. And because of your good manners, I'll throw in for free their Shadow Guardian, Figment," he said, magically producing a robed figure of about six inches high from the folds of his billowing cloak.

As soon as the old man mentioned the name Figment, darkness quickly descended over the entire area of the fair, blocking out what little sun there was, quickly followed by a roll of thunder that could be heard in the distance. Seconds later fork lightning flashed across the skies and thunder crashed once more with so much force the ground shook under my feet! I stood rooted to the spot in shock, scratching my head, trying to work out what was going on. The feeling was 'spooky' to say the least.

Then, as rapidly as it had appeared, the darkness mysteriously vanished, leaving a cloudless blue sky, and leaving me to wonder whether everything that had just happened was just a 'figment' of my imagination.

"Weirdness isn't the word. I couldn't even begin to describe what had just happened to me just then."

"What the heck was that all about?" I asked the old man, craning my neck, searching the skies for the rain clouds. By this time my whole body was churning with nervous tension.

He didn't answer me straight away, due to the fact that he was scanning up and down the line of stalls with his beady eyes. It seemed as though he was looking for someone in particular. After a few jittery seconds, he placed the tips of his fingers up to his lips and whispered, "Let's just keep our voices down for a little while, shall we? We wouldn't want any unsavoury characters suddenly appearing." Once again he was closely inspecting the faces in the distance with his probing eyes.

I didn't bother questioning him, because everything that was going on around me didn't make any sense at all. It was complete and utter madness! Also, I wasn't entirely sure if I'd heard him correctly. It was then that I thought it might be best if I humoured him, as he didn't look as though he was any kind of threat.

"What the heck is a Shadow Guardian?" I inquired, licking my chapped lips and wrapping my coat around my shivering body.

"You may find it more comfortable if you came around to this side of the stall. It will only take me a few minutes to tell you everything you need to know about the Tree-Spirits and their Shadow Guardian," he answered, shuffling around in his chair, attempting to find me some room.

"Thank you for the kind offer of a seat mister, and I don't want to offend you, but I've been told by my parents hundreds of times not to be too friendly with strange men. And if they find out, they'll go mad and they won't let me play out for weeks."

"You haven't offended me young man. And I suppose you don't see too many strange characters like me hanging around these days. Now where were we, oh yes, I remember now.

"First, let me enlighten you about the Shadow Guardian, and then I will tell you what you need to know about these two particular Tree-Spirits. Oh, by the way, the male spirit is called Aticuss, and the female is called Fay. Now please listen very carefully to what I have to say. It's very important."

The old man then paused for a few seconds to gather

his thoughts.

"A Shadow Guardian is an exceptional faerie that has the ability to control its size. At will, they can become immense in stature or magically shrink down to the size of a teeny-weeny speck of dust. They can also drastically alter their appearance, assuming any guise they may desire. I've heard say that there are Shadow Guardians out there that are more powerful than others. These particular ones boast the power to transform the appearance or size of other faeries and more worrying, mere mortals like ourselves. But not to worry; I haven't had the honour of coming across any of those in my travels – not just yet anyway!"

"Then how do you know this particular Guardian isn't one of those powerful ones?" I asked. I was now eager to hear what he had to say.

"That's the strange fascination of being in the *presence* of Tree-Spirits and their guardians. You never know when you will come into contact with one of the 'Gifted Ones'," he replied, grinning and nodding his head slightly as though I knew what he was going on about.

"I'm not entirely sure, but I'm pretty certain he also winked at me."

"I suppose I'll have to take your word on that, won't I? ... Whoa there, just hold your horses, will you? The way you're describing Figment, it's as though this individual is alive and kicking. Yet it's only a silly doll stuffed with old newspapers and strips of prickly straw, wearing old tatty clothes," I pointed out to him. "Isn't it?" I added, waiting for an answer with bated breath.

A wry smile crossed his face which caused me to

shiver, and that wasn't from the biting cold wind that had suddenly sprung up. Anyway, it was at that worrying stage when I decided it would be a good idea to take my leave.

"I must be going. I've been here long enough, and Mum and Dad will be worried sick. Goodbye, and I hope you manage to sell some of your weird decorations."

"Please let me finish, I beg you. I know you want me to, I can see it in your eyes, and it won't take me long, I promise," the old man said, once again rubbing his grey wrinkly hands.

"Go on then, but be quick about it. I've been hanging around here for ages," I snapped back, scanning the dozens of faces around me for Mum and Dad. There was no sign of them at all, which was disappointing, because if they had shown up, they could have helped me get away from this screwball.

In the meantime the old man had got himself nicely settled on his stool, and he'd continued with his bizarre fairy tale.

"What I'm about to tell you is very important, so take note and please concentrate on what I'm saying. Okay?" he ordered, in the same tone and authority as my English teacher.

"I'm listening," I snapped back. Yet I have to say, I was now bursting with curiosity.

"You MUST always ensure the Tree-Spirits are close to their Guardian so he can watch over them day and night if not the Shadow Thief will appear, which I can assure you it certainly will. This would give the Shadow Thief the opportunity to steal the Tree-Spirits and their shadows. If that happens, heaven forbid, you must recover them with utmost urgency." He stopped for a few seconds to get his thoughts back into some semblance of order. I used the

15

opportunity to my advantage, as I was now becoming anxious to check out the other stalls.

"What's all this talk about some nasty Shadow Thief? You're talking in blooming riddles. I only came to the fair with my Mum and Dad to buy some stupid Christmas tree decorations... " The old man cut me off mid-sentence by frantically gesturing with a wave of his hands in the air for me to stop. It worked, and he looked clearly agitated and annoyed by my interruption.

"Be silent young man, and just listen to what I have to say. I've now come to the most important part; do you understand?" he snapped back at me.

Nodding my head like an idiot, I inched my way closer to the stall so I could hear him more clearly. The tone of his voice told me that it was no use in arguing, so I kept quiet, at the same time trying hard to rub some warmth into my cold hands.

"If Nanny Buttoncap, that's the name of the nasty Shadow Thief by the way, captures the Tree-Spirits, and more importantly their shadows, and then for some unworldly reason you don't return their shadows to them before Twelfth Night, Aticuss and Fay will be compelled to live forever 'in between' in the twilight regions; 'The Middle Kingdom' ... and young man, you could never imagine in a million years what will happen to them, and where they will eventually end up ..."

I was now beginning to regret coming down to the stall in the first place. I should have tagged along with Mum and Dad. Never mind, I thought. What the old man was going on about was utter rubbish. There are no such things as Tree-Spirits, Shadow Guardians and especially Shadow Thieves. The guy must be on drugs or else he'd been smoking some wacky-backy before I'd arrived.

At this point my mind was so mixed up with what I'd been hearing I hadn't realised, but he'd started once more with his unbelievable far-fetched fairy tale.

" ... She guardedly stores away the thousands of shadows she's taken in a worn out leather pouch that's securely fastened around her person. She also methodically catalogues all of the names in a very remarkable leather-bound journal, 'The Book of Tormented Shadows', and mark my words young man, that is *ONE* evil, magical journal you definitely don't want to find your name listed in. Because if by some wretched accident that did happen ... are you listening to what I'm saying, or am I boring you? It's essential that you take note; if not, you will regret it for the rest of your life. Do you understand?" he shouted angrily, causing me to step back in alarm.

By now, I was shivering from the cold and also becoming annoyed with the old man's ranting and raving. So with that in mind, I gathered up the box with the two Tree-Spirits, tucking it under my arm. I grabbed hold of their Guardian, carefully slipping him into my coat pocket, and tossed my ten-shilling note across to the old man.

Not forgetting my manners, I thanked him for the decorations, stepping away from the stall. In an instant, the sounds and smells suddenly attacked my senses, causing me to reach out and grab the wooden upright of the stall over to my right for some means of support. I then had an unusual feeling as though I had been woken up from a deep, deep sleep. I felt groggy and light-headed. Blackness swam before my eyes. I then began to wonder if that was an out-of-body sensation I'd just experienced, because over the last hour, I definitely didn't seem to be in my mind or body.

I began to raise my worried body, shaking my head, hoping to clear it. I glanced up, peering at the scores of people milling around me. It was then, to my sheer horror and disgust, that I caught sight of a number of weird-looking gruesome creatures staring directly back at me. They appeared to be drifting aimlessly amongst the shoppers. The bodies of the creatures seemed to be made from a dirty grey mist that floated just inches from the ground. Yet for some unexplained reason, none of the other shoppers were taking any notice of them!

I staggered back, tearing my eyes from the horrible creatures, focusing on the ground. I started to lose my balance as the illusion distorted my mind, so I closed my eyes and held my head in my hands. I began to shudder with fright as I rubbed my eyes, hoping to rid the gruesome images of the hideous creatures. "Just pull yourself together will you, Barnaby," I told myself, trembling with fear.

A few panicky seconds later I finally plucked up the courage to open my eyes a crack, slyly peeping at the swarm of people, eyes shifting left and right. To my joy, there was no sign of any of the beasts, or whatever you want to call them. It must have been my imagination running riot, or the dizziness I'd just experienced. To tell you the truth, nothing would have come as any surprise to me just then after my wacky encounter with the odd gentleman.

Satisfied it was safe to move on, I hastily threaded my way through the hordes of sweaty shoppers, searching for Mum and Dad.

I'd only walked a short distance when I came across

them. Luckily, they had their backs to me, so they hadn't spotted me approaching them.

"Well, here goes," I mumbled under my breath, my fingers tightly crossed. No doubt I'm going to be punished for being missing for so long. Yet I knew they wouldn't cause a scene in public. They'd wait until we were back home.

"Please don't shout at me. I'd completely lost track of time, but I did buy some awesome Christmas decorations for the tree." I began to shuffle my feet a few inches away from them, as I didn't want a clip around the ear-hole from Dad.

"Hi son, what are you doing back here so soon? I thought you said you wanted to spend some time in the fair all by yourself," Dad asked, ruffling my hair.

"What do you mean back so soon? I've been gone for flipping ages. Well it seems that way to me." "What's happening to me," I thought. Am I ill? Because I'm pretty certain I was at the stall for at least half an hour, or even more. Anyway, I knew there was no point in arguing, so I kept close to them both as we barged our way through the crowds of people, noticing that most of them were lugging bulging shopping bags, fit to burst. Why do people always leave it to the last minute to buy their pressies?

"Well, did you manage to find something to spend your money on, Barnaby?" Mum asked, glancing down at me.

"Yes, I bought two amazing Tree-Spirits and their Guardian. And you know what both of you? I was reliably informed by the stall holder that all three are supposed to bring you good luck over the Christmas period," I said, peering down at the wooden box that was wedged tightly under my arm.

"I know, I know, the part about the Tree-Spirits giving us good luck was a little white lie. I didn't have the heart to tell them the whole truth. Also, I don't think they would have believed me — would you?"

"Come on then, Barnaby, let's see what you've bought. One thing's for sure, if what's inside isn't much cop, the box will be worth a pretty penny, don't you think Mum?" said Dad, trying to ease open the lid, with no success.

"Do you have the key, Barnaby, it seems to be locked?" Dad asked. Sweat was streaming down his face, which he brushed away with the back of his hand.

"It's not locked. Here Dad, let me take a look." You should have seen the shocked expression on Dad's face when the lid snapped open with ease when I touched the top of the box.

"Wow! How much did you pay for these Barnaby? They look like they could be worth a fortune, and they seem really old," inquired Dad, carefully inspecting Aticuss in his shaky hands.

"Please be careful. Dad, they're very fragile, and I wouldn't want you to drop them on the floor and break them."

"Don't worry son, I can see how delicate this one is. Here, take it off me before it slips out of my trembling fingers, and make sure you put it safely back in the box. Where did you say the stall was? I'd like to go and see it for myself, it sounds really interesting," said Dad, gingerly handing Aticuss over to me.

"It's this way, just around the corner, by ..." I stopped mid-sentence, shuddering to a halt, because to my alarm, where the stall should have been, there was now an old rusting van resting on four flat tyres.

"This can't be happening. I must be dreaming," I thought, as I wandered up and down the line of crowded stalls, checking out the stallholders. Or is my mind playing tricks?

"Are you sure you've come to the right place, Barnaby? All the stalls look alike, don't you think?" asked Mum, wrapping her arm around me, gently squeezing.

"Yes, I'm certain. I can remember the smelly cheese stall directly next to it. Just hold on a minute both of you. I'll go over and ask the woman serving at the cheese counter. She's bound to remember the old man selling Christmas decorations in the stall next to hers."

I nervously stepped up to the cheese stall, at the same time mopping away the sweat that had appeared on my brow with my handkerchief, even though I was shivering from the cold.

"Excuse me, lady. I wonder if you could help me please. A few minutes ago I bought some Christmas decorations from an old white-haired gentleman in the stall directly next to yours. Did you happen to notice where he went?" I asked, indicating with a wave of my hand towards the spot. From the puzzled expression on the women's face I knew I wasn't going to get the answer I was hoping for.

"Sorry lovey, there hasn't been any kind of stall on this side of me all day; only this great hulking piece of junk that stinks of grease and oil," she said, gesturing with a nod of her head towards the rusty old van.

"You must be mistaken. It was only a few minutes ago when I bought some Tree-Spirits from the stall. You must have noticed him. He was an odd-looking character. He wore a brown cloak, and his stall was covered with an array of brightly-coloured Christmas decorations. Please think hard lady, it's very important."

"Sonny, I may be old and in the prime of my life, but I have all my faculties, and I am damn sure that there has been NO fancy stall with a hooded gentleman next to mine. So I would suggest that you go home and have a happy Christmas with your family."

I didn't bother discussing it any further with her, because she had already turned her back on me, and was now in the process of serving an old man who I'd noticed had been listening intently throughout our conversation.

"Come on Barnaby, we've been at the fair long enough, and it's now getting cold enough to snow. And don't let it worry you. You must have got yourself all muddled up in all of the excitement of buying the Tree-Spirits," Mum said, ruffling my hair. "Let's head off back home ... and I'll tell you what, I'll pop a few mince pies in the oven. We can have them for tea along with some nice ice cream. What do you say to that?"

I wasn't really bothered about the mince pies or the stupid ice cream. I just wanted Mum and Dad to see the mysterious-looking stall and the weird old gentleman for themselves.

Whilst reflecting on the past few extraordinary minutes, the nosey gentleman who'd been buying the smelly cheese and ear-wigging stepped directly in front of me, blocking my path. In the meantime, Mum and Dad had moved to the next stall, inspecting some weird wooden toys.

"Please don't be alarmed. I won't keep you very long from your family, I promise, but it's imperative I talk to you," he said, leaning a little closer to me so that he wouldn't have to raise his voice. He also put his hand on my arm, closing his fingers on my wrist.

"Get off me, please," I said, trying desperately to pull away from his grasp.

He quickly released his hand, and I jerked my arm away in a flash.

"Sorry about that, I don't know my own strength, but you see, I don't want you to run off as I must talk to you," he said, looking embarrassed from his actions.

I took a step back and began to rub my arm, at the same time accepting his apology with a nod of my head. I then positioned myself on the balls of my feet just in case I needed to leg it.

"Do you know what? I wouldn't have been surprised if he'd confessed to being a Big-Wig-Wizard, and he could magically make himself disappear into dust by just clicking his fingers. My brain was now in overdrive. I was also eager to hear what 'he' had to say."

The old man grinned at me, his teeth blinding white. "I couldn't help but overhear your bizarre conversation with the cheese lady. You see, I bought two Tree-Spirits and their Guardian some fifty years ago from the same old gentleman, and I'd be really interested to hear what he had to say to you. Would you mind telling me?" he asked, cocking his head to one side, shuffling from one foot to another as though he was in a hurry.

How could I not tell him? Also, I desperately wanted some answers to the weird information I'd just been given a short while ago.

It took me all of five minutes to reveal to him what I knew, leaving him to sigh and shake his head.

"Can I see the two Tree-Spirits and their Guardian for myself? I won't take them off you, I promise," he asked, smiling, holding out his hands, fingers flat, palms up.

I swallowed and stared hard at him for a moment. "I'd

23

rather not, if you don't mind. I've become quite attached to them in the short time they've been in my possession," I replied, wedging the box safely under my sweaty armpit and then thrusting my right hand deep into my coat pocket, ensuring Figment was still safely tucked away at the bottom.

He'd left his hand extended for a moment, before slowly slipping it into his coat pocket. He didn't look too happy. In actual fact, he seemed downright mad. Tough, both the box and Figment are staying with me, thank you very much.

Do you know what, reader? There was something not right about him that made the hairs on the back of my neck stand on end, followed by dozens of goose bumps sprouting all over my arms. So I gritted my teeth, waiting patiently to hear what his response would be to my refusal. Also, his eyes disturbed me. There was something unsettling in them, something evil. His eyes began to flicker over me, from head to toe, as though he was taking a mental picture. To my surprise he smiled, although it did look forced, then he shrugged his shoulders. He then continued talking.

"You must make certain you take notice of everything the old man said to you. If not, your life will become unbearable. Unfortunately, I didn't follow his instructions to the letter. I thought it was all poppycock. At first, I kept all three safely together on the Christmas tree in our front room. Then a few days after Christmas, I decided to take their Guardian to my mate's house to show him off to him. That's when my unearthly problems began. You see, somehow The Shadow Thief, Nanny Buttoncap, sensed that their Guardian had been separated from the Tree-Spirits, and she sneakily found a way into my house

24

and stole the Tree-Spirits' shadows." He paused awhile, and once he'd got his emotions in check, he carried on.

"I hadn't a clue where to start looking for Nanny Buttoncap. So I just accepted the consequences, waiting nervously for the mayhem to begin after Twelfth Night. Now my life is a misery. I can't leave the house for more than thirty minutes at a time. If I'm away any longer, I know that in my absence the furniture will be destroyed, and it will also give the Tree-Spirits the opportunity to escape from the house. If that happened, I couldn't even hazard a guess what the outcome would be. I don't know if you are aware young man, but the myths and legends about faeries are many and diverse. Yet there is only one thing that is clear — nothing is clear, as all things are possible in 'The Land of Faeries' ..." He then paused awhile, trying to get his composure back.

"Please take my advice son, I beg you. Make sure you position the Tree-Spirits safely on your Christmas tree along with their Guardian. Watch over them day and night with your life until Twelfth Night, especially their Guardian, and then you can release all three to the greenery where they belong. If you do all that, you and your family will be safe."

What have I got myself into? I only wanted to buy some stupid Christmas decorations, yet now I am being told in no uncertain terms that my life may be in danger if I don't follow some ridiculous instructions. It was at that particular frightening stage when I seriously considered handing over the box and Figment to the gentleman, and then at least my worries would be over and done with.

I began to rock back and forth, shaking my head, trying to weigh up my options. But to be honest with you, it didn't take me long to decide to keep all three. They felt as though they were part of me now. Friends, if you know what I mean.

"I'm aware that it's going to be very difficult for someone of your age to come to terms with what I've just disclosed to you, but please, please believe me ... and while I think of it, here, take this. It will protect you, just in case you come into contact with the countless number of nasty little people, or 'The Wee Ones' as they are commonly known," he said, handing something over to me that looked like a tree root.

"What is it?" I enquired, closely inspecting an odd-looking dark brown root that had small purple pods attached to the sides.

"Snake-root. If you find yourself in a tight spot with any of The Wee Ones, crush the pods with the tips of your fingers. The toxin from the pods leaves a bitter odour that sends them mad. But use it sparingly; snake-root doesn't grow in our world."

"Our world, what the heck do you mean by that? ... Ouch!" I screamed. Flashes of red-hot pain instantly shot up through my hand to the base of my neck. "Hey mister, one of these funny pods on this root thingy has bitten the back of my hand." I took a deep breath, grimacing and licking the sweat from my upper lip. Tears burnt into my eyes from the pain, and a sudden pang of nausea washed over me.

I hastily began to examine the small wound, finding something like a thorn embedded in the meat of the gash. I quickly used my chewed-down fingernails, trying to pull out the thorn. Yet the more I tried to pull it out, the more the thorn dug deeper into my swelling hand. Panicking, I dragged my thumbnail across the ends of the pink flesh, trying to snag the thorn out. But the more I dug, the deeper the thorn went. Another hot wave of nausea swept over me as I tore at the wound, making it bigger. It was then that I decided to stop, as the thorn had disappeared into the leaking wound. My hand and arm began to tingle like crazy, similar to when you whack you funny bone.

I quickly began to focus on my breathing, struggling to clear my head, whilst dabbing the back of my hand with my nice clean handkerchief.

Because of the harm it had done to me I flung the snake-root onto the floor before crushing it into tiny pieces with the heel of my shoe ...

Fortunately for me, my concentration was broken. Mum was calling me over, ordering me to hurry up and stop dawdling. And I was just about to give the nosey old man a piece of my mind when I realised he'd mysteriously disappeared. He'd vanished into thin air. No blinding flash of light, no puff of smoke and flame, just gone.

"Come on Barnaby, you've been watching too many 'B' movies again at the cinema on a Saturday morning," I thought, as I made my way towards the smiling faces of Mum and Dad. Unfortunately, it was the soreness on the back of my hand that brought me back to earth!

Satisfied my precious box was safely cradled under my arm, and Figment was carefully arranged at the bottom of my coat pocket, I joined Mum and Dad. We made our way to the exit, once again fighting our way through the crowd of people who were making their way home.

You know what? The more I thought about what the frightened old man had just said to me, the less I believed his story. Firstly, he started off by being kind and friendly, giving me advice. Then he became mad and furious with me when I'd not show him the Tree-Spirits and Figment. Then, out of the blue, he gave me that stupid snake-root.

Weird toxins that send The Wee Ones mad if you crush the pods? A likely story!

I thought it would be best not to raise the encounter with the old man with Mum and Dad. Those facts would be best kept to myself, for the time being at least. But to be honest with you, I felt as though I was letting them both down by not discussing it with them. After a few anxious seconds weighing up the alternatives, I kept my mouth shut. And I certainly wasn't going to say anything to them about the gash on the back of my hand, as I knew Mum would only fuss over me, insisting that she takes me straight over to the hospital to be checked out by a doctor. Anyway, the pain had eased a little, and I knew in time my body should reject the thorn like any normal splinter. But I wasn't all that confident. You see, there was something not right about the whole episode with the nosey old man. As I was peering into his hypnotic eyes, I thought I saw something flicker in the man's face as he stared back at me. And at one frightening point, just for a split second mind you, I could sense a rippling effect spreading across his whole body, from head to toe, similar to a heat haze shimmering on a baking-hot road. I then suddenly shuddered, remembering the awful images of those hideous-looking creatures that had blended in with the rest of the unwary shoppers.

After arriving safely home, thankfully without anything untoward happening to my family or me on the way, Dad proceeded to plant the Christmas tree into a cut-down metal dustbin. With Mum, once again giggling away to herself, complaining about all the soil Dad was constantly dropping and treading in all over the living room carpet.

Some fifteen minutes later, Dad had the tree carefully planted in the dustbin, and was now in the process of stringing up the Christmas tree lights.

While all this was going on, I'd eased Figment out from the pocket of my coat and cautiously took the Tree-Spirits out of their box; placing all three carefully in the centre of the dining room table.

It was when I was turning to face the Christmas tree that I thought I saw something out of the corner of my eye; some slight twitch of motion from one of the three dolls. I blinked and stared at them, cautiously reaching out with my shaky hand, poking all three with the tip of my finger. They didn't move or stir, which didn't come as any surprise. They were only dolls stuffed with shreds of old newspaper and scratchy pieces of straw, I reminded myself.

"I must be more tired than I'd realised," I thought, rubbing my eyes.

"Come on Barnaby, what are you waiting for? The tree is all ready to hang up the decorations," Dad said, fussing over the tree, ensuring it wasn't going to fall over. It didn't look too secure for my liking, so I made sure I didn't pull the branches too far forwards as I hung the tacky assortment of decorations up first. I then picked six thick, sturdy-looking branches, before carefully positioning my three hand-made decorations on so they wouldn't slip and fall off, followed by the Tree-Spirits and their Guardian.

It was now getting late, and I was shattered from the frightening ordeal I'd had at the fair. Also, I wasn't too bothered about staying up late to watch the telly. So I said goodnight to Mum and Dad and clambered up the stairs to my cold bedroom. It didn't take me long to clean my teeth, change into my pyjamas and climb into bed.

I was finding it difficult at first, trying to fall asleep. I was totally exhausted. My mind was racing around like a hamster on an exercise wheel, working like mad, but getting nowhere. Too many hideous images and revolting thoughts were running through my muddled brain. Once again I was going over in my head the weird conversations I'd had with the two gentlemen. I suppose I should have realised at the time that something wasn't quite right.

"I certainly hope I don't run into them again," I thought, massaging the back of my sore hand.

Propping my big fluffy pillow up against the head of the bed, I eased myself back, supporting my head with my hands, and turned over in my mind the amazing accumulation of information I'd heard, and also all that I'd witnessed during the course of the afternoon ...

"I'm sorry, but I'm going to have to take a short break, and it's starting to get dark out there as the night closes in ... 'Out there'. To be honest with you, I've got no idea what out there is anymore. These are strange lands I've found myself in, inhabited by unnatural and loathsome creatures ... also the light's beginning to fade rapidly, and I'm finding it hard trying to see what I'm writing; the words are just blurs in front of my tired, watery eyes.

"Once I'm certain there's no nasty individuals hanging around, I'll light one of my treasured candles and start again. So please be patient with me..."

Chapter Four
24 December Midnight

Anyhow, I must have fallen asleep, because the next thing that I remember was when I woke up sweating, even though all of my blankets had ended up on the bedroom floor, and in the distance, the distinctive sound of church bells striking midnight.

Christmas Day. "Yippee."

"What's that noise? It sounds as though it's coming from downstairs." "Not to worry," I thought, Mum and Dad must be still up. "Oh no, they're not, I can hear them b-both talking and giggling away in the next r-room," I was stuttering from the cold.

"Don't be so silly Barnaby. The noise must have been coming from somewhere outside," I told myself, leaning over the side of the bed, groping around on the floor in the dark for my blankets. On second thoughts, it might be best if I went downstairs to investigate. You never know, someone may be trying to steal the Christmas presents from under the tree. Yet I have to say, that was highly unlikely, as vandalism and break-ins were rare in our neighbourhood.

"Oh no. There it goes again!" I croaked, trembling with fear.

My imagination was now running overtime as I hastily collected my crumpled up clothes from the foot of the bed.

Struggling to tuck my shirt down into the top of my jeans, and panicking may I add, I once again heard the unnerving sounds coming from downstairs. At that frightening stage I thought it might be best if I jumped straight back into bed and bury my head under the covers until daylight. On second thoughts, why don't I just go and wake Mum and Dad up, and make them aware of the strange noises that are coming from downstairs?

"Nah, I don't think I'll bother. They'll probably shout at me for disturbing their sleep, order me straight back to bed and tell me not to be so silly," I thought, trying to put on a brave face.

After a few jittery seconds, I made up my mind to go and check out what was going on one floor below.

Before easing the door open, I placed my right ear against the bedroom wall, trying to determine whether Mum and Dad had gone to sleep yet. Not a sound, thank goodness, and surprisingly, Dad wasn't snoring. The only sounds I could hear were the wind and the groaning of the branches from the big oak tree in our next-door neighbour's garden, combined with the sounds of my heavy breathing.

Certain there was no likelihood of Mum and Dad coming out to investigate the noise I was making on the landing, I stealthily made my way down towards the foot of the staircase, carefully positioning my stocking feet at both sides of the stairs so as not to make any of the wooden floorboards creak under my weight. I was also trying to be as quiet as a mouse, and shaking with fear, not knowing what to expect.

"There it goes again," I mumbled to myself, wiping away the sweat from the palm of my hands down the front of my sweater. "And it seems as though it's coming from the front room?" My heart was pounding like a jackhammer in my chest, and I had to stop myself a couple of times from crying out for Mum and Dad.

I crept one slow nervous step at a time toward the foot of the stairs. Nearing the bottom, I noticed a mixture of bright coloured lights outlining the foot of the living room door, laying a swath of gold and red across the floor of the hall.

"Dad must have left the Christmas tree lights on," I thought. I then stopped short when I unexpectantly heard voices, at least a pair of them, talking in hushed, urgent tones, coming directly from the front room.

Could it be that Aticuss, Fay and Figment have come to life? "Don't be so stupid," I chastised myself, tiptoeing toward the door. Sweat chilled my spine. I was dreading the next few minutes.

"Well there's only one way to find out, isn't there?" I was scared out of my wits. I surprised myself that I'd found the courage to go on. Yet I carried on anyway.

After taking a deep breath, I hastily wrapped my sweaty fingers around the handle and pushed the living room door open with a jolt. The door opened a crack, and squeaked. I quickly stepped inside. Another annoying squeak came from the door, loud enough for Mum and Dad to hear if they'd been awake. I held my breath, listening. It took a few seconds for my eyes to adjust to the sudden darkness of the room. Oh, oh, the lights on the tree weren't switched on at all. "So where did that weird light come from?" I wondered, trembling with fear.

My eyes began to dart from one side of the room to the other. I breathed out, quickly fumbling around on the wall for the light switch with my right hand. I found it and flicked it on.

"I know there's someone hiding in here, so show yourself this minute. If you don't, I'll go straight upstairs and wake my parents up," I declared, panicking.

I then eased the door shut behind me, once again nervously scanning the room.

By now, the fire had died down to glowing embers, but it still shed a small amount of red-golden light over the room, thank goodness.

"Was it the glow from the fire that spilt out beneath the door?" I thought, at the same trying to convince myself it was that all the time.

I quickly began to fish around inside my jeans pocket for my sturdy pocket-knife that I'd picked up from my bedside table whilst getting dressed. What use that was going to be was anyone's guess. Anyway, it made me feel a little bit braver if nothing else.

The room felt deathly quiet, save for the remains of the cinders that were spitting and hissing from the constant rainfall coming down the soot-coated chimney.

For a couple of minutes my whole body was paralysed with fear, and my tongue stuck to the roof of my mouth. I just stood there like an idiot, listening to the worsening rain outside and the sound of thunder in the distance. I daren't move a muscle, or utter a single word. It felt as though unseen eyes were watching me. Goose bumps formed all over my body, my shirt stuck to my back, and my heart almost missed a beat. Then it suddenly dawned on me; if there were someone hiding in the room, what would I do when faced with them or it?

Whilst I was mulling over in my mind the various frightening possibilities, to my astonishment and utter amazement, there slowly emerged from behind the tree — causing it to lean to one side — what I can only describe as three extraordinary human-shaped creatures.

My jaw dropped to the floor, and I held my breath. I tried to speak, but nothing came out, only the breath I was holding. I was totally spell bound, and my heart started to pound a little more quickly with fear. I struggled to say something, but my mouth didn't work.

Yet I knew without any shadow of a doubt, that the three, just feet in front of me, were the Tree-Spirits and their Guardian, Figment. And, for some strange reason, their clothes had changed from when I'd placed them on the tree just a few hours before.

Yet that was the least of my worries. What was more disturbing and frightening was the fact that I had three alien creatures sneaking around my front room.

"Don't worry Barnaby, you'll wake up in a minute?" I thought. But to my utter bewilderment, I didn't, because I knew that what was happening before me was real all right!

Not one of us moved an inch. I certainly couldn't talk. My jaw was nearly touching the floor. Eyes like dustbin lids. I studied them for a few seconds in silence, listening to the clock on the mantelpiece counting down the seconds.

On closer examination I noticed that Aticuss and Fay's faces were partially hidden by bright red hoods attached to long flowing coarse robes that reached all the way to the carpet. And on their small feet were green sparkly, pointy shoes that peeked out from beneath the hem of their robes. This made me smile. Figment on the other hand was robed in hand-woven sackcloth, belted with string that looked to be plaited from plants; his feet were shod in rough animal skins. He wore a well-worn dark brown hood, which obscured the top of his face.

Some awkward minutes later, it was Figment who broke

the unearthly silence, peeling the hood away, revealing a strong face, a full head of white hair and a long white goatee beard.

"I'm so sorry we have woken you up. It was never our intention to disturb your sleep. You must have very sensitive hearing, or it may be no coincidence that you have caught us red-handed as you mortals like to say. The vast majority of humans cannot hear or sense us; only the gifted ones can ... you must be special. But be not afraid Barnaby Tinker-Tailor, we mean you no harm. All we ask is for a safe haven in your house until Twelfth Night, and then we shall be on our way."

I remembered it as though it was yesterday. His voice was so soft, the tone strangely melodic and soothing. I just wanted to lie down and curl up in a ball and fall fast asleep.

It was the sound of a car backfiring outside on the main road that brought me out of my dreamlike state.

"You've g-g-grown to my s-s-size," I stuttered. "And how on earth do you expect me to keep you three well hidden until Twelfth Night, now that you are my size?" I asked, staring at the unbelievable vision before me.

Then to my complete shock, Knuckledown, Rosie Apple and Tickety-Boo suddenly appeared from behind Aticuss's shoulder.

"What the ..." I gasped, taking a step back from their unexpected appearance, in the process stumbling into the dining room table, banging my shin on the corner. "Damn that hurt ... And how come you three have come to life and grown to my size as well?" I groaned, hobbling around the room, rubbing my bruised shin and trying to keep my voice down at the same time. This wasn't an easy feat, I can tell you.

Suddenly I felt light-headed, excited and terrified all at the same time. My throat constricted, and if I hadn't been holding my breath, I think I would have let out a throaty cry.

"Am I tucked up fast asleep in bed, and I'll wake up in the morning remembering nothing of this bizarre dream as usual?" I asked myself once more.

"No, I'm most definitely awake, because I could hear Mr. Croad coughing and sneezing next door. Can't he sleep; doesn't he ever go to bed?" I thought, feeling nervous and frightened.

Once my head had cleared, I limped over toward the fireplace for some warmth, as it had suddenly turned cold in the room. I then slumped down heavily in the chair nearest to the dying fire. Then taking care not to make too much noise and wake up Mum and Dad, I cautiously placed a handful of coal onto the fire. Sparks chased up the chimney as I fanned the flames, and soon I had the fire blazing away. The flames leapt up the chimney, throwing red shadows across the room, giving off some additional welcoming light. I then turned in my chair, glancing back over my shoulder at what I could only describe as a weird assortment of 'things'.

"Barnaby, because we are all safe and secure in your house, I feel it is only right that I tell you a little about the World of Tree-Spirits — *our* world. In simple terms, it's an alternative world that exists parallel to yours. And I think you will find it very interesting. Believe me Barnaby, most humans do.

"I am fully aware that you already know about Nanny Buttoncap, the Shadow Thief, from the wise old man you bought us from at the fair. You also need to know that I am the last of the Shadow Guardians, and Nanny Buttoncap will move Heaven and Earth to capture me. She is a wicked, wicked person, and she takes great pleasure in stealing the shadows of the Tree-Spirits when the opportunity arises. She also has many fearful friends, which you need to be aware of, such as the Spriggans and Sylvans. All of these faerie folk are evil and spiteful, but her closest friends you need to be mindful of are 'The Unseelie Court'. These are thoroughly evil creatures; they appear in groups at night and live mostly on the wild and windy moors. They're also known as 'The Host' and they fly through the air snatching up any mortal unfortunate enough to fall in their path. Please heed my words Barnaby Tinker-Tailor. Nanny Buttoncap is also Shape-Changer. This means those close to you may not be as they seem."

"How am I expected to know who I'm talking to then?" I asked, panicking. Sweat began to trickle into my eyes; I brushed it away with the tips of my fingers.

"Look very closely at her eyes, Barnaby. Nanny Buttoncap never ever blinks. Eyes are the windows to your soul, Barnaby. You won't see a soul in Nanny's eyes; she doesn't even know the meaning of compassion and love," answered Figment, stepping toward me, his brown robe whispering around his legs. He made himself comfortable in the chair opposite.

I let out a pent-up breath, dropping my head into my hands. My mind was in utter turmoil. I couldn't take it all in. Here I was, sitting in my front room, talking to a mish-mash of curious looking beings, whilst Mum and Dad were innocently sleeping upstairs. I was absolutely dumbstruck, and it took me a while to clear my muddled brain.

In the meantime, I'd observed that my assortment of makeshift decorations had moved a safe distance from the side of the wobbling tree.

On closer inspection, I noticed to my bewilderment that Rosie Apple and Tickety-Boo had sylph-like bodies; pointy ears and large slanting eyes. Rosie Apple's crudely-made paper wings had been replaced with a pair of dazzling colourful butterfly wings. I also spied an array of colourful beads and shells strung around her delicate-looking neck, and she had the most kindly green sparkling eyes I'd ever seen. Partly hidden under her robe was a glistening blue dress that looked to be studded with stars from the night sky. Upon her head was a faerie crown of twinkling stars, and held tightly in her right hand was what I could only describe as a luminescent crystal wand that sparkled from the many stars that adorned her.

Tickety-Boo also looked completely different from last night. Her hair was unnaturally long and luxuriantly golden. It looked to have been blown about in the wind. She had a pair of gauzy-type wings, similar to dragonflies', which stretched out behind her as though she was ready to take flight. Her dress was white and looked as if it could have been made out of light, for it radiated pure white light. I instantly fell in love with them both. I didn't take much notice of Knuckledown at that stage as I was once again drifting about in a dream-like state, mesmerised by the two radiant female creatures standing in front of me.

Saying that, I definitely knew I wasn't asleep, because I felt a sudden pain on the back of my hand from my fresh wound and I could feel the warmth from the fire caressing the side of my clammy face. I could also make out the dim amber glow of the streetlamps through the lace curtains hanging in the front bay window.

After a few minutes I finally plucked up the courage to question Figment.

"Figment? In addition to the earth-shattering instructions the wrinkly old stallholder gave me, I bumped into an odd gentleman at the fair. He told me that he'd bought two Tree-Spirits and their Guardian from the same old man some fifty years ago. Regrettably, he didn't do as instructed. At one stage, their Guardian became separated from the Tree-Spirits. Consequently, Nanny Buttoncap stole their shadows. Figment, I need to ask you a very important question. If, by any chance, you become separated from Aticuss and Fay, or their shadows are taken from them, will they change into mischievous faeries?" I felt it wouldn't be the right time to raise the incident with the snake-root with him just at that moment.

By the look on his face, it looked as though it was going to be difficult.

A heavy silence followed, before Figment flexed the fingers of one hand, popping his knuckles, "An odd-looking gentlemen, you say, would you please describe him to me, Barnaby."

I knew I had to keep a cool head and not give anything away. But that's easier said than done, especially facing a wizard, or whatever you want to call him.

"To tell you the truth Figment, I don't remember too much about him. By then, I was so excited with buying you three. Just wait a minute though; there was one thing I did notice which I thought was odd at the time. When I was listening to him, and staring into his creepy eyes, I felt as though I was looking at more than one person. His whole body seemed to ripple like a lace curtain blowing in the wind." I felt it was only right that I told Figment a little bit about the old man to check out his reaction.

"I wished I'd kept my mouth shut!" I thought, turning away from his probing eyes.

"Oh my, oh my. Barnaby, I'm pretty certain that was Nanny Buttoncap. Did he ask to see us three, or by any chance did he give you anything, anything at all?"

"Such as?" I asked, slyly sliding my hand down the side of the cushion of the chair so he wouldn't spot the wound.

Figment cleared his throat and looked at me oddly. "Barnaby, please don't play silly games with me. This is deadly serious — did he, or did he not, give you anything?" he repeated, angrily.

"No, he didn't. Once he'd finished going over his stupid story, he vanished into thin air, which I thought was also odd at the time. Anyway, what could he have given me that was so important, and why are you so concerned about him wanting to see the three of you?"

"Barnaby, handing us over to him of your own free will would have meant that Nanny would have been able to control us. And you definitely wouldn't have seen us again. Anyway we are all safe, thanks to you. But in the meantime, I'll have to take your word that you didn't take anything off him ... her, or whatever you want to call it. But please don't meddle with things that may harm you. Whilst we are all safe and warm in your house, nothing will happen. Yet there are things out there which you wouldn't want to get mixed up with. Trust me on that Barnaby Tinker-Tailor."

"Just hold on a second will you Figment? If what you say is correct, and that old man I bumped into was Nanny, how come he, or whatever you want to call it, warned me about protecting the Tree-Spirits' shadows? It doesn't make any sense at all. He came across as someone who was trying to be friendly, not any kind of threat. Also, when I come to think about it, why didn't IT just buy you three at the fair when he had the opportunity? That's if he wanted the Tree-Spirits' shadows so desperately," I enquired. I was now becoming eager for some answers, and I was also becoming concerned about the thorn that was slowly digging its way deeper into my skin.

"She was only toying with you Barnaby; playing silly games and giving you a false sense of security. And the answer to your question about why didn't Nanny buy us from the old man ...when you were standing up close to the stall, did you have the weirdest feeling ever, as though your whole body was cocooned ... trapped in a world all of your own? No sound, no smells?"

That's when I nodded my head like a complete idiot, gazing into his hypnotic eyes. "The night was getting spookier by the minute," I thought, raking my fingers through my dishevelled hair.

"Barnaby, whilst you were at the stall you were being protected by a faerie force field which Nanny couldn't penetrate. That meant she couldn't get anyway near us, and if she'd made any kind of attempt to reach and grab us, she would have been forced back with a jolt, similar to a massive electric shock, killing her. Barnaby, there is only one thing that is clear in all of this — nothing is clear, as all things are possible in the 'World of Faeries'," he added.

Oh dear, what have I got myself into? If I remember correctly, the bit about everything not being clear was what that Nanny what's-her-name mentioned to me. Should I now confess everything to Figment, including the snake-root, or do I keep my mouth shut?

By now the throbbing in my hand had eased a little, so I decided to keep my little secret to myself. Yet, from the disbelieving expression on his face, I could see Figment

42

didn't trust me. "That's his problem," I thought. But to tell you the truth reader, I wish I had been totally honest and told him everything. I can assure you of that.

Figment then began to shuffle around in his chair so as to make himself more comfortable before continuing.

"I hope I haven't scared you Barnaby? But not all Tree-Spirits are wicked. Actually, some of them are quite fun when you get to know them. As faeries go I mean. Barnaby, has there ever been a time when you have put something down, only to find it missing when you've gone back to pick it up, and then you find it someplace else? And how many times have you heard your Mum and Dad ask if anyone's seen the front door keys, informing you that they'd left them on the hall table and they've now mysteriously disappeared. Then, after spending minutes searching around on top of the mantelpiece and down the back of the couch, they were on the hall table all the time. Well, these are childlike faeries. They won't harm you or do any lasting damage to your home. They just like clowning around."

"When I come to think of it, yes, that's happened to me and my family on a number of occasions. But I've never had Tree-Spirits in the house before, so how come there were faeries in my house then?" I inquired, excitedly.

"These are the young mischievous faeries that have somehow escaped from Nanny Buttoncap's grasp, and they're just having a bit of fun. They won't harm you anyway. You can take my word for it. Barnaby, you've had a great deal of faerie knowledge to take in. I would suggest you go back to bed and get some sleep and we'll meet up again tonight, once we are certain your parents are fast asleep. But before you go Barnaby, there is one very important point you need to know. When you are in the presence of faeries, or 'The Good Folk' as we prefer to be known, you are also in The Land of Faeries. This means time slows down. In fact, minutes can pass in our realm, which are equivalent to whole years in the human world. That's when it suits us," he added with a wink and a cheeky smile.

I whistled through the gap in my front teeth before taking a deep breath. "Figment, do you mind if I ask you a silly question?"

"Go ahead, and just remember Barnaby, true friends don't keep secrets from one another. That means I could never tell a human a lie if I tried," he said, looking sheepishly at me as though he knew *I* was keeping something from him. I held my nerve for a few seconds before continuing.

"Where is 'Fairyland'?" I asked. I was now anxious for some answers. And the excitement bubbling up inside me was causing my whole body to tremble with anticipation.

"Barnaby, Fairyland is said to be somewhere just over the horizon, and somewhere beneath our feet. So close, no matter how far. When in The Land of Faeries no luggage is required, no passport or travel insurance is needed. Check-in time is nil, and arrival time is ... well, just a wish away. Faeries are able to move from their realm, Fairyland, freely to your world, as they inhabit both, and so are able to see us as part of their natural world. The Land of Faeries is to many people a symbol of childhood dreams; a place of hope that signifies that magic may still exist; where glamour, beauty and fairy tales are eternal. It's also a place not of this world, so it can't be considered to have a physical location on any map. There are special doorways known as 'faerie portals' where we can reach Fairyland from this world of ours. It's an exceptionally

44

beautiful place where the light is constantly dusky; a place where the sun never rises or sets but a place of 'in between' as if forever spring. But be aware; it is easy to get trapped in The Land of Faeries ..." his voice trailed off, leaving me with my mouth hanging open, slumping heavily back in my chair.

After that piece of mind-boggling advice and faerie knowledge, Figment eased back in his chair, staring up at the ceiling, eyes tightly closed.

Just then, Fay forced her way to the front of the group, a look of concern spread across her angelic face, "Can he be trusted to watch over us, Figment? He's so young and innocent," she asked, scrutinising my surprised-looking face.

"Just hold on a minute will you. What do you mean can *I* be trusted? I should be asking you that same question. It isn't everyday I find an assortment of weird looking characters in my front room?" I responded angrily, shaking my head from the insult that had been thrown at me.

In a flash, Figment spun around in his chair, addressing them all in a strange language. From where I was sitting, I couldn't make out a single word he was saying.

After a few nervous seconds there was a murmur of agreement, followed by the nodding of heads and they began to relax a little. Fay then glanced across and smiled at me, her eyes sparkling from the light seeping in from outside. At that point I slowly eased back in my chair and relaxed, with the feeling that they had all accepted me. It was then when I felt guilty for not mentioning to Figment about the pod of the snake-root worming its way into the back of my hand. Can't be any worse than a common-or-garden splinter I reminded myself. "Or could it?" I thought despairingly.

"Now, please listen to my counsel, Barnaby. If you have a small bell, I would strongly suggest that you find it, and keep it somewhere safe in the house. This will aid you in scaring any evil faeries away from your home. Also, I would recommend that you place a filled saltcellar in the centre of your kitchen table. These two important pieces of advice will keep you and your family safe from the meddlesome attentions of any nasty faeries that may appear."

There it goes again, the dreamlike sensation of floating around in the air when Figment opened his mouth. And what's all that about bells and salt? I thought I was in the presence of faeries, not vampires with leprosy? Anyway, I had no intentions of questioning Figment about these quirky lucky charms and horrible bogeymen and women just at that moment.

Over the past few years I'd read numerous books at school about faeries and hobgoblins, yet would you believe it? Standing right in front of me, in my little old house, was an assortment of six magical creatures. But, for some unknown reason, I didn't feel threatened by or frightened of any of them. Yet how did Figment expect me to settle and go back to sleep after what I had just witnessed and digested over the past half hour? I was also keen to know how Knuckledown, Rosie Apple and Tickety-Boo came to be living and breathing in my front room. It must be another kind of weird spell from Figment. But wait on ... the white-haired old man at the stall told me about certain faeries who had the power to transform the appearances of other faeries and mortals. I wonder if Figment was one of those ...?

I don't know what actually occurred after that, but the next thing that I remember was when Dad came barging into my bedroom, wishing me a happy Christmas and jumping up and down on my bed like a complete fool.

"Dad, will you stop it? You're going to break my bed. And just watch where you're putting your feet, you nearly landed on my legs just then," I screamed.

Luckily, Dad had run out of breath before any serious damage had been inflicted on the bed, and more importantly, on my legs.

During all of this silliness, I had managed to safely crawl out of bed. Meanwhile, Dad had collapsed on his back on the bedroom floor, chuckling away to himself and gasping for air.

"Come on Dad, will you get out of my bedroom so I can get dressed? I'll see you downstairs by the tree, unless it's fallen down during the night, it didn't look safe to me last night ..." I suddenly stopped mid-flow, remembering my unearthly encounter with Figment and the others just a few hours before. I began to panic. A nervous knot formed in my stomach. I knew without any shadow of a doubt, Mum and Dad would easily spot them hiding behind the Christmas tree. They must be blind as bats if they didn't.

Luckily, I could hear Mum downstairs in the kitchen, singing to a Christmas carol that was playing on the radio. But where had Dad disappeared too? Great, I can hear him in the bathroom. Right, now's my chance to run downstairs and see if there's some place where I can hide the six of them. I knew straight away that there was no way I would be able to find a hiding place for them all in the front room, especially with them being human size. Let's hope all six of them have reverted back to their normal size, then there may be a slim chance of them not being spotted.

Once dressed, I took the stairs three steps at a time,

landing heavily at the bottom with a thud on my backside.

"Barnaby, how many times do you need telling about hurtling down those stairs? One of these days you're going to injure yourself. So don't come running to me when you've broken both legs." I could hear Mum chuckling away from her silly remark. I wish I had a penny every time she came out with that statement. I would be a millionaire by now.

"Well, at least I can't hear any movement in the front room, thank goodness," I muttered under my breath. I then lifted myself up from the dusty floor, brushing away the dust from the seat of my pants.

After easing the door open, I quickly stepped inside. Certain the door was shut; I began to search behind the Christmas tree for the odd-looking creatures. Nothing, or 'zilch' as Dad would say.

"Where are you hiding? I can't see any of you," I whispered, checking behind the curtains.

"We're safely back in the tree in our original guise. I have the magical powers to make us all change size when the need arises," came the soothing voice of Figment from within the greenery of the tree.

That surely meant that Figment is one of those powerful faeries, and also a shape changer. If that's the case, how the heck will I know if he is what he says he is? There's only one sure way to find out – look into his eyes.

Before doing that important task, I quickly dashed back to the door to check out what Mum and Dad were getting up to.

"Cool." Mum's still in the kitchen, and I can hear Dad splashing about in the bath. I've at the most ten or fifteen minutes before one of them comes into the room. That meant I couldn't afford to mess around for too long. I then recalled what Figment had said about time slowing down when you were in the presence of Faeries. Well, there was no way I was going to risk Mum and Dad finding any of them; so I started to move a number of large gift-wrapped Christmas presents from the base of the tree to one side so I could get closer. With very little effort I managed to pull the branches apart without too many needles falling to the floor or dislodging any of our crappy decorations. It was the sudden sight of the three spirits and my hand-made decorations precariously balancing on the prickly branches that made me catch my breath.

"Crikey guys, you scared the hell out of me then." I could hear my heart pounding in my ears. Once my nerves had settled, I asked Figment if I could look in his eyes.

A friendly smile passed over his face. The crafty faerie knew what I was up to. "You are a wise boy for your age Barnaby Tinker-Tailor."

Sitting cross-legged on one of the prickly branches, Figment, to my relief, blinked a number of times to show me that he was who he said he was. I also noticed that the others were giggling and shuffling around, trying to find a more comfortable place to sit and relax.

"Figment, while I'm standing up close to you, there won't be a problem examining your eyes. So what happens when I can't see them? I could be talking to Nanny What's-her-name without realising it," I asked, deep in thought.

"Good thinking Barnaby, and do you have any ideas what to do?" asked Figment.

After concentrating for a few seconds, I recalled something Mum had mentioned to me about Dad before I was born. "What we need is a password?"

"Excellent Barnaby. Any suggestions, and make sure it's simple; we don't want to forget it, in a crisis?"

"Yes I have. When Mum was nearing the end of her pregnancy with me, Dad had weird cravings for boiled eggs and piccalilli, so when I can't see your eyes properly, I'll call out boiled eggs, and you can answer me back with Piccalilli. Okay?" I said excitedly. Figment looked up into my eyes, shook his head, and chuckled under his breath. "Whatever you say Barnaby. If it makes you happy."

"Barnaby, don't you open your presents until we've all had breakfast. Can your hear me in there?" called out Mum from the kitchen.

"I won't Mum, don't worry, I'm just going to watch Tom and Jerry," I called back, smirking with pride.

Well, I thought despairingly, how are these six going to be quiet and not move around all day, especially with my cousin Isobel coming over in the afternoon for Christmas tea? I knew for a flipping fact the first thing she will do when she arrives will be to go snooping around the tree searching for the fancy chocolate decorations. I know what I will do. I'll hide those in the pantry, and then she may not bother with the tree when she sees there aren't any chocolates to take off. I certainly hoped so.

Certain my new friends were safe and secure, I began to carefully rearrange a few of the decorations on the tree, in the vain hope that no one would spot the six of them if they just happened to be walking past. Also, I wasn't entirely certain, Figment may have the powers to change them all into small specks of dust. If that's the case, I hope Mum doesn't decide to Hoover the carpet and fuss over the tree.

By 10.0am we had opened all of our presents, with Dad leaving the big one for me until last as usual. As I was flicking through my Dandy Annual, Dad wheeled in my new bike. I had a hunch they'd bought me one for Christmas and I was right.

"Wow, thanks!" I screamed, dropping the book to the floor, springing to my feet.

It was awesome. It had red and yellow criss-crossing stripes running up and down the frame. And, to my delight, it had five gears and drop handlebars. Great, at last I had a big boy's bike.

Unfortunately, it was still pouring down with rain, so there was no way I was going to try out my new bike and get it wet.

Just in case you are interested, I bought Mum a smelly bath set in a brightly coloured box, all tied up with a fancy purple ribbon. The box contained a large tube of talcum powder, some bubble bath salts and a big bar of pink smelly soap.

Since starting buying Christmas presents for my parents, I had always found it difficult trying to think of what to buy Dad. This year I bought him a pen and pencil set. He seemed to be impressed with it.

After all the hugs and kisses were over, we collected the torn wrapping paper from the floor and tossed it into the roaring fire Dad had lit whilst we were opening our presents. I then gingerly manoeuvred my bike out of the front room and into the kitchen, resting it against the kitchen table.

"Oh crap. It's still raining! Never mind, I will just have to be patient that's all. At least I have my other pressies to play with."

"Language, Barnaby," came the booming voice of Dad

from the front room, followed by a chuckle.

"Sorry Dad." I called back, giggling away to myself ...

"I'm going to have to stop writing for a while as my hand is becoming numb from the cold. It's so cold; my pen keeps slipping from my fingers ...

" ... Ah, that's much better. A few minutes sat on your cold hands certainly does the trick. Also I've managed to find a pair of fingerless woollen gloves. They were in one of the drawers in the back room. There're probably from the last tenant. That's the good news. The bad news is that I'm totally out of food and water. Not a measly crumb or a drop of water! Not to worry, I've been in worse situations than this ..."

Chapter Five

Christmas Day 3.00 pm

I don't know if your family are the same as mine on Christmas day, but 3 pm on the dot we all have to quietly sit down in front of the TV and listen to the Queen make her customary Christmas speech to the Commonwealth.

"Yuk!"

Luckily for me, I had only been watching the programme for a few minutes when there came a knock on the front door.

"Go and answer the door for me please Barnaby, and let the Jones tribe in while I go and find somewhere to hide all the chocolates before they get their greedy hands on them," said Dad, shoving his half-eaten packet of salted peanuts down the side of his chair with one hand, whilst at the same time sneakily sliding an unopened box of Milk Tray under the couch with his other.

"George! That's my sister and her family you're talking about. Just you behave yourself," snapped Mum, playfully slapping Dad on his shiny baldhead, giggling.

After inviting the three guests into the house, I quickly took their coats from them before scampering up the stairs to Mum's bedroom. Flinging the pile of coats on top of the bed, I noticed that a couple of them had landed on the floor. I had no intentions of picking them up, as I needed to be downstairs, fast.

"What did Father Christmas bring you, Barnaby? Mum

and Dad bought me a new record player along with the Beatles' Sgt. Pepper album," squealed my cousin Isobel, heading over in the direction of the Christmas tree, no doubt looking for the chocolate decorations. You're going to be one disappointed young lady I thought, smiling over at Dad. Dad returned the smile and winked.

"Mum knitted me a gruesome sweater. Sorry Mum, I meant a fantastic sweater. They also bought me an awesome bike, but I haven't been able to use it yet, because it's been raining most of the day. I got lots of other boy's things, but I don't think you'd be interested in any of them." I replied. It was then when I could have kicked myself. If she'd wanted to go to my bedroom to see the other presents I'd put up there, she wouldn't go snooping around the tree.

"You blooming idiot," I muttered under my breath.

"Who are you calling an idiot, Barnaby, I hope that wasn't directed at me?" asked an angry Isobel, stamping her feet on the carpet like a spoiled child.

"Don't be so daft; I was only talking to myself. Why don't we go to my bedroom? I've a large selection box we can open, and you can have the first pick." I was hoping that would keep her mind off other things.

"Barnaby, don't you go making yourself sick eating all of your chocolates. We'll be having tea soon," Mum informed me, smiling.

"Don't worry Mum, I won't," I replied, gesturing with a sweep of my hand for Isobel to leave the room ...

Isobel and I have definitely nothing in common as far as appearances go. Where I am small and stocky, she is tall and lean. Where I have black wavy hair and baby-blue eyes, she's got long chestnut hair and dark brown eyes. Where my features are wide, with a small button nose, hers are smooth, with the kind of cute nose you'd expect to see on a stick-thin model ...

By 7 pm we had all stuffed ourselves with a hearty meal of chicken, spuds, greens and loads of thick lumpy gravy that Dad had made. It was followed by the traditional jelly trifle Mum always makes at Christmas, all smothered in Carnation milk. Great ...

"Goodnight George and Barnaby, and a happy new year to you both, and we hope to see you in the spring when we all go camping," shouted Auntie, after giving Mum a big hug and a sloppy kiss on both cheeks.

As she was slowly making her way down the garden path toward the gate, I couldn't help but notice Isobel secretly clutching something very close to her chest, and gazing back over her shoulder at me, smirking like the cat that had got the cream. It was then when I had an awful feeling at the pit of my stomach. Oh no! She must have taken something, and it can't have been the chocolate decorations, because I'd hid them all in the pantry.

I turned and sprinted to the front room, quickly striding over to the tree, nervously easing the branches to one side, searching for my friends.

There were only four of them huddled together! Aticuss and Fay were missing. My mouth fell open. I broke out in a cold sweat, and I felt as though someone had wrenched my heart out of my mouth. Somehow, Isobel had managed to sneakily steal the Tree-Spirits from under my nose, but how and when I asked myself?

Then I remembered her drifting over by the tree when we were all watching The Morecambe and Wise Christmas Show. The reason I remembered so clearly was because my bladder was full and I had to go to the bathroom. I should have hidden the six of them in the wardrobe in my bedroom. They would have been much safer in there. What on earth am I going to do now?

"Barnaby, that was very rude of you, running off without saying goodbye to your cousin. And what's got into you today? You've been wandering around the house like a cat on a hot tin roof. Are you coming down with something?" asked Mum, resting the palm of her hand on my forehead.

"Your skin feels slightly warm to the touch. You may have come down with something, or it could just be your age. Boys," laughed Mum, shaking her head.

What could I say? There was no way I was going to mention Figment and the Tree-Spirits, not forgetting Knuckedown, Rosie Apple and Tickety-Boo. She'd go ballistic and order me to get them out of the house that minute.

"Sorry Mum, it was the call of nature, and I couldn't wait any longer. Here, let me help you clear the table." I said, trying to work out how I was going to get the Tree-Spirits back home. Also, the thought of Nanny Buttoncap appearing at any moment caused me further heartache.

I quickly began to closely scrutinise Mum's eyes, as I didn't want any more nasty surprises. Not to worry, she was blinking and wiping her eyes with the corner of her tea towel.

 Once the table was cleared, I left Mum and Dad in the kitchen to wash up. In the meantime, I had stealthily crept back over to the Christmas tree, and it didn't come as any surprise to me when I peered between the branches only to find four sullen faces staring back at me.

"What are you aiming to do now, Barnaby? You're our only hope of getting them back," enquired Figment, resting his chin in his hands, sighing. "Also we need to be extra vigilant. Nanny Buttoncap will now sense that the Tree-Spirits are not in my protection anymore."

Just the mention of her name sent a chill through my bones.

"What do you mean, what am *I* aiming to do? I'm going to need all the help I can get. And why on earth didn't you stop Isobel from taking Aticuss and Fay? Especially with you being some kind of freaky magical faerie and all," I demanded, once again panicking at the thought of Nanny Buttoncap appearing in the house. I then spotted Figment shuffling along the branch, no doubt making himself comfortable before giving me some more mind-boggling advice.

"Barnaby, can you imagine what the reaction would have been from the members of your family if I'd somehow prevented Isobel from plucking Aticuss and Fay from the tree? The repercussions would have been catastrophic. We must all be patient, and until then we will have to rely on your help and cunning in getting them safely back to me."

"You've got to be joking! Who do you think I am, The Lone Ranger? And how on earth do you expect a twelve-year-old boy to overcome the enormous 'might' of The Shadow Thief and all of her frightening minions? Just hold on a second will you? Can't you magic yourself back to my size? That way we may have a slim chance of overcoming Nanny What's-her-name." I was now becoming excited knowing I may have solved the problem.

"I'm sorry to be the bearer of bad news, Barnaby, but there is a faerie code I must follow to the letter. You see, while I'm in the safety of your home, there is no problem at all transforming to your size. But once I set foot outside of the house, I have to revert back to my normal height.

Sorry."

"Come on Figment. Couldn't you bend the rules just a tiny bit? I'm pretty certain no one would be any the wiser. You've got to admit, it is for a special cause." I was praying my begging would make Figment feel he had to take some responsibility. I was also trying to keep my cool.

An uneasy silence spread across the room as Figment considered my suggestion, and it was some minutes before he looked up. The sad expression on his face instantly told me that my pleading had been a complete waste of time.

"Barnaby, I wish with all my heart that I could change things as you've asked me to do. The reason why I can't 'bend the rules' like you've requested, is that as soon as I transfigure myself to your size and step outside of the house, Nanny Buttoncap will know my whereabouts. And that is the last thing we want at this crucial time. There is also a limit to how much I can involve myself in mortal affairs. But not to worry, Barnaby; I am more powerful and useful as I am now." Figment then moved away, slumping down heavily on a thick prickly branch, once again resting his head in his hands.

"Oh Jeez, what an almighty pickle I've got myself into," I thought, closing my eyes for a second, contemplating my next move.

It was the sound of the kitchen door opening, followed by Mum calling out to me, which interrupted my troubled thoughts.

"Barnaby, will you come into the kitchen and finish off the drying for me please? Dad's got a stinker of a headache and he wants to go and lie down on the bed for a while."

"Okay Mum, I'll be there in a minute." I let out a breath of frustration and rubbed my eyes before wiping away the build-up of sweat from the palms of my hands down the sleeves of my jumper. A sickly feeling of dread washed over me.

Before stepping away from the tree, I instructed all four to be very still and patient, and wait for me until morning.

"I'll figure a way of getting them back to you all, don't you worry." The only problem was, I hadn't the foggiest idea how I was going to do that. No doubt I'll come up with something — I certainly hope so!

"My eye-lids are now becoming heavy, and I have a headache starting right at the back of my eyes. I need a wash. I stink. Yet I'm not surprised, after being on the run in this indescribable world in the same old threadbare clothes. Also, I need to be ready to leave at a moment's notice.

"You may be interested to know, I dreamt about Mum last night. She was making breakfast, and telling me about a game she played as a child with her brother and sister, about running away and hiding in the garden from monsters. Then I woke up with the characteristic smells of bacon sizzling in the frying pan, combined with the aroma of freshly buttered toast. I didn't dwell on it for too long as it made me sad ...

"Anyway, once I'm feeling refreshed, I'll begin writing again."

Chapter Six

Boxing Day

It was a long restless night, and I tried numerous times to relax and go to sleep, hoping to erase everything that had happened to me over the past twenty-four hours. But it was useless. Once again I was panicking, wondering whether Nanny Buttoncap may appear during the night, disguised as Mum or Dad. My mind was utterly confused!

Resting my head on my pillow, gazing up at my World Cup Poster, I tried to come up with a plan. A million different thoughts swam around in my head ... the images of the two old men at the fair, along with those disgusting grotesque creatures circulating around those unsuspecting innocent shoppers. Plus I had the added worry of the painful thorn slowly burrowing its way deep beneath my skin, and I think my hand may be infected now. It's gone from sore when I touch it, to a steady throbbing pain!

After drifting on and off to sleep, I eventually came up with a plan. The best bet, I thought, would be for me to go over to Isobel's house first thing in the morning and confront her face to face. I knew at that stage I would have to tell her everything about the Tree-Spirits, and especially Nanny Buttoncap. So let's hope she doesn't cause a scene and blabs about it to her parents. Anyway, I thought it a good idea at the time.

I don't know how long it took me to fall asleep, but eventually I did ...

My eyelids snapped open with a start, my legs kicking and flailing my sheets and blankets around the bed. My whole body was coated in sweat and repugnant images of twenty-foot black-scaled monsters with sharp dripping fangs swam before my eyes. My jumbled mind was trying to work out if all that had happened to me the other day was just an awful dream. Slowly but surely, my surroundings came into focus, and sadly; it was the dull ache on the back of my hand that told me that I'd just had a nightmare.

It took me a few tense seconds to slow my breathing down. Sweat was still pouring down my face, which I wiped away with the corner of my creased bed sheet.

Once composed, I glanced over toward the bedroom window, noticing through the lace curtains that it was starting to get a shade lighter outside. I then rolled over to check the time on my Mickey Mouse alarm clock on my bedside table. The illuminated hands were fixed at 8 am. I quickly leapt out of bed and threw back the curtains, checking out the weather. Great. The rain clouds had finally passed and I could actually see some sunlight peeking intermittently through the thick white clouds that were slowly drifting overhead.

Wiping away the build-up of condensation on the window with my hand and gazing at the early risers taking their dogs for a leisurely walk, I felt somewhat uneasy and unsure as to whether I was doing the right thing, calling in unannounced at Auntie's house.

Knowing there was no alternative, I began to quickly pick up my discarded clothes that I'd slung on the floor the night before and got dressed, at the same time listening out for any kind of movement from Mum and Dad's room. Not a murmur, thank goodness!

Satisfied I'd piled on enough warm clothes, I carefully

tore a page out from one of my school textbooks, hastily scribbling down a note for Mum and Dad. I informed them that I didn't want to disturb them; it had stopped raining and I was going for a ride on my new bike. I told them not to worry as I would only be gone a short while. I was hoping so.

Certain Mum and Dad weren't about to suddenly appear from their bedroom, I tiptoed nervously down the stairs to the front room, where I knew my worried friends would be patiently waiting.

The front room was eerily quiet and gloomy, save for the radio blaring out Christmas carols from next door. "The walls in these houses must be made of cardboard," I thought, pulling back the curtains for some additional light, then cautiously inching my way over toward the Christmas tree.

I eased the branches carefully apart to check out where my little group of warriors were. And, as I'd expected, they were all slumped together on a thick branch, staring back at me in a frightened state. Even my hand-made decorations seemed to be somewhat agitated, which surprised me, as their shadows weren't at risk.

It was Figment who spoke up first. "Piccalilli, and did you manage to come up with any ideas to get Aticuss and Fay back to us?" he asked, amused by his own wit, and shielding his eyes from the strong winter sunlight piercing the room.

I didn't answer him straight away because *I* was also chuckling away to myself, at the same time carefully examining his piercing eyes. They looked to be all puffy and red like mine. Probably from lack of sleep, I presumed. But the most important thing was he'd said the password, and he was blinking.

"You remembered the password, and I'm supposed to say boiled eggs first. And yes, I have a plan. I'm going to go straight over to my Aunt's house on my bike and hopefully get them both back from my nasty cousin Isobel. Let's just hope she doesn't get too upset and decide not to give them back to me. She can be really mean when she sets her mind to it. Anyway, we'll just have to cross that bridge when we come to it won't we?" I asked them. By this time we were all giggling away like children.

"Sssh, keep your voices down will you, you'll wake my parents up." I said, tears streaming down my cheeks. We all knew it was a worrying time, but the laughter did ease some of the tension in the room. Then I don't know what came over me, maybe because I was feeling somewhat happy and more relaxed, but I thought it might be best if I took the four of them along with me. So when I do eventually get the Tree-Spirits back, they will be safe and well in the protection of Figment. The only problem was, what do I carry them around in? My school duffel bag was probably the best bet. It was large enough for them all to settle down in some comfort, and I'd tuck some nice clean towels in at the bottom to make it warmer and a bit cosier for them whilst they're being jostled around.

"If it's all right with you lot, I think it may be best if you tagged along with me to keep you out of harm's way. The last thing I want right now is for Mum and Dad to come across you four while I'm out there looking for Aticuss and Fay. I can use my school duffel bag to carry you around in, and I'll pop some clean fluffy towels inside so you won't end up hurting yourselves ... so get that worried look off your faces, and sort yourselves out, while I go and collect my duffel bag from the kitchen."

I wasn't in any kind of mood for arguing with Figment,

or any of the others for that matter, so I carefully eased the branches back into place before heading of out of the room, carefully closing the door behind me.

Pausing at the foot of the stairs, I tried to detect any kind of movement from Mum's bedroom. Silence. No doubt they will be sleeping off the sherry they were drinking throughout the course of the afternoon and night. I'm not surprised Dad had a stinking headache. "Serves him right," I chuckled under my breath, making my way to the kitchen.

After collecting my duffel bag from the pantry, I slipped a couple of bottles of pop and an unopened packet of Rich Tea biscuits into the side pockets. I then carefully propped my handwritten note up against the salt cellar on the kitchen table so it wouldn't slip off onto the floor; they're bound to see it when they walk into the kitchen. I then pulled out two sweet smelling towels from one of the kitchen drawers along with an old cat's collar we'd been storing in there for years. The collar had a small bell attached to it. And after Figment's comment about a bell being useful for scaring off evil Faeries, I thought I'd leave it resting up against the salt cellar along with my note so as to give Mum and Dad some additional protection whilst I'm out of the house.

Once I was happy all four were comfortably settled at the bottom of the duffel bag I carefully zipped up the pocket, ensuring there was enough space for them to see what they were doing; also making sure they didn't run out of air. And when I was satisfied that the duffel bag was securely strapped around my arms and shoulders, I unlocked the back door. I turned off the lights to the kitchen and sneakily wheeled my bike outside into the cold morning air, locking up behind me. The air was damp with the smell of trees, of nature, and in the distance I heard a faint rumble of thunder. The storm was returning.

Making my way anxiously down the garden path I stopped to glance back at the house I grew up in, wondering if I'd ever see it again. My stomach churned with anticipation, not knowing how Isobel would react to my unexpected appearance, especially at this time in the morning. I was also terrified, wondering if Nanny Buttoncap may appear in some form of disguise before I safely reached Isobel's house. I was also hoping I didn't bump into any of those ugly creatures I'd spotted at the fair ...

Chapter Seven

Boxing Day

I couldn't remember the last time we'd visited Auntie's house, which meant I had to stop a number of times on the way to think where she lived. What I did know, the last time we went by bus, and if I remember correctly, it only took us fifteen minutes and that was with four stops. With that in mind I knew it couldn't be too far away.

The cold blustery wind was making my eyes water, and my teeth began to chatter as I pedalled like fury up and down the steep winding hills, my duffel bag banging against my back. My ears felt as though they were blocks of ice. Yet there was one consolation about all of this; my bike was flipping awesome, especially having the five gears to aid me.

Twenty-five sweaty minutes later, fighting against the onslaught of the blustery cold wind, I eventually arrived by the front gate to Auntie's house, relieved. From where I was standing, it looked as though no-one was up and about yet. The curtains to the living room and the front bedroom were tightly drawn and there was no clear evidence of smoke rising out of the chimney.

"Never mind, I know what to do," I thought, trying to look as though I was calling in on an errand. The last thing I wanted right now was some nosey-parker neighbour assuming I was about to break into the house, getting on the phone and reporting me to the police.

Without further hesitation I eased open the front gate and wheeled my bike down the path by the side of the house toward the back garden before carefully slipping the duffel bag from my shoulders, resting it on the garden wall and unzipping it.

Peering down into the shadowy interior of the bag, ensuring the four hadn't been injured in any way by my jerky movements from my frantic pedalling, I spotted four sets of wide eyes staring back up at me.

"Are we there yet?" asked Figment, rubbing his eyes and shuffling around, trying to position himself in a more comfortable place. "And have you any idea how stuffy and cramped it is inside here?" he added, shielding his eyes to the sudden glare of the morning sun.

"Yes, we've arrived. The only problem we have is that there doesn't seem to be anyone up and about yet. But if I remember correctly, Isobel's bedroom is at the back of the house. So once I'm certain there aren't any busybodies peering out through their bedroom windows, I'll toss some small stones up at her window. Hopefully that will attract her attention and wake her up. In the meantime, make yourself as comfortable as possible, and I will update you as soon as I can. Okay?"

I didn't get a reply from any of them, only muffled mumblings from deep within the dark interior of the bag. On reflection, they couldn't object anyway. I was helping them out after all.

Parking my bike close to the side of the dustbins, I then carefully eased the duffel bag onto the floor, just behind the front wheel of the bike so it couldn't be kicked over by accident. And then, after collecting half a dozen small stones from the border of my uncle's prize-winning garden pond, I stepped onto the carefully manicured lawn, preparing myself to throw one of the stones at the window.

It was then when I had a horrible thought. What if I was wrong, and my aunt and uncle were now sleeping in this bedroom? Well, there's only one way to find out, isn't there? "Here goes," I whispered nervously, pulling back my arm, launching the first stone.

"Crickey, Moses," I cried out in alarm. I thought the glass was going to break when the stone struck the window. Because of the noise I'd made, I hastily scanned the windows of the dozens of houses that backed onto the garden, looking for any signs of twitching curtains. Nothing. Mustn't be light sleepers around here, thank goodness.

"Well, if there is anyone sleeping in that bedroom, there won't be anymore after that racket," I told myself, cupping my hands and blowing into them to keep warm, because for some unknown reason, the air was turning colder by the second.

"This is getting weirder and weirder," I remembered thinking at the time, shivering.

I didn't have to wait too long in the cold before the curtains were thrown back with a bleary-eyed Isobel glaring down at me through the misted-up bedroom window. In a matter of seconds she swung the window open, before shouting down at me. Her face was like thunder.

"What the heck are you playing at, Barnaby? You nearly broke my bedroom window just then. And what are you doing in my back garden at this time in the morning? Can't your family sleep? Your Dad was here about fifteen minutes ago, banging on our front door, demanding that I give him back your stupid Christmas decorations. And before you start telling me off, I've already apologised to him, so I don't need another blooming lecture coming from the likes of you. Also you'll be happy to know, I handed the stupid dolls back to him, so clear off, and goodbye."

My mouth suddenly became dry. I stood rooted to the spot. How could Dad have been here before me when it had only taken me just over twenty minutes to get to Isobel's house on my bike? Also, I left Dad fast asleep in bed when I'd left the house. That's unless he'd heard the sound of the back door being closed when I'd sneaked out of the house.

I think I know what may have happened. He must have gone down to the kitchen to investigate the noise I'd made and found my note on the kitchen table. But wait on; I never mentioned anything in the note about going over to Isobel's house. Oh no! It wasn't Dad who was here a few minutes ago. It was that Nanny Buttoncap person, thingy, what's-her-name, scary Shadow Thief!

"Haven't you gone yet?" she called out, leaning her slim five foot five frame out of the window, her long dishevelled hair blowing about in the cold blustery wind.

"Can I come into the house for a few minutes? And I promise I won't go on about you taking the Tree-Spirits from the tree?" I pleaded, hoping the four hidden deep in the duffel bag hadn't overheard Isobel's confession.

"What are you going on about you silly boy? And what the blooming heck is a Tree-Spirit ... that's what you said isn't it, Barnaby?" she asked, giggling away to herself, before slamming the window shut, causing the glass in the frame to rattle.

"Please let me come inside Isobel so I can explain everything properly to you," I called out in despair, hoping she'd heard me before she'd closed the window.

I spun around and quickly began to search the shadows of the bushes and trees in the back garden for any signs of movement, as there was a strong possibility Nanny Buttoncap may still be lurking around. I hoped not! The only sound I could hear was the tall oak trees creaking and groaning beneath the wind. Then a chill ran down my neck. I was pretty certain that someone was out here in the darkness; I could feel eyes on me. I squinted into the shadows of the garden, sweeping my gaze slowly around. I could see nothing. But I would have bet money that there was someone out there watching me. My mouth tasted like cardboard and my tongue stuck to the roof of my mouth. I was now desperate to get into the house and I was also panicking, not knowing what Nanny would do to me if she caught me. I tried desperately to wash that scary thought from my befuddled brain ...

Then to my sheer joy the back door flew open, with an angry-looking Isobel gesturing for me to quickly step inside the house, holding the door open, trying to stop the warmth escaping from the kitchen. All of a sudden, a loud roll of thunder that seemed to go on for ages could be heard in the distance, which made us stop what we were doing. We both stood frozen on the spot by the open kitchen doorway, scanning the sky for the dark rain clouds. Yet the sun was bright, and the sky was the colour of eggshells. Once again thunder crashed across the skies from all sides, followed by a number of blinding white flashes that lit up the sky and our immediate surroundings. I quickly ducked down, covering my face, worried that I was going be struck down by a lightning bolt.

Shivering with fear we both quickly stepped inside the house, slamming the door shut behind us and releasing a pent-up breath we'd both been holding. You know what, just for a split-second before dashing into the kitchen, I had an awful feeling that someone was watching us from within the inky shadows of the trees and bushes positioned at the bottom of the garden. I shivered from the thought.

Because of the weird situation I was about to put her in, I thought it best not to mention that to Isobel. I didn't want to frighten her, and I knew the next few tense and frightening minutes were going to blow her tiny mind! So I kept my mouth shut, pulled out a chair from under the table and plonked myself down.

"Barnaby, what on earth is going on with you and your family?" asked Isobel, cautiously easing the kitchen curtains to one side, slyly peeking out through the window into the back garden.

"Let's sit down." I said, using my toe to poke the facing chair out from under the kitchen table.

"Just hold on a minute, Barnaby, I'll make some strong coffee first; I think I'm going to need it after *that* weird experience."

A couple of minutes later she sat down across from me with two mugs of steaming hot coffee and an opened packet of digestive biscuits.

"So?" she asked, rolling her eyes and tut-tutting. She had a nasty habit of doing that, which always wound me up, and she blooming well knew it. For once, I didn't bite, as I had other important matters on my mind.

"Barnaby," she continued, "those weird decorations I took off your tree last night must be pretty important for your Dad to come around and disturb my family at that unearthly time in the morning."

"Where do I begin?" I thought, shrugging my shoulders and rubbing my tired eyes.

I stretched out my legs, took a deep breath and braced myself for her reaction. "Unearthly is probably the best description of what's happened to me over the past twenty-four hours. Please sit still and be quiet for a while, so I can explain to you why I'm here. Also, that wasn't my Dad that called in to see you this morning. It was a horrible Shadow Thief called Nanny Buttoncap. I know, I know, it sounds far-fetched. So I suggest you drink your coffee and listen to what I have to say, and then you can decide if you want to help me out or not, especially with you putting me in this precarious position in the first place."

"Barnaby, I know I'm not your favourite cousin, and I do tease you now and again. And as you know, I can also take a joke, but this has gone far enough. So drink your coffee and then go and spend some quality time on your new bike whilst it's stopped raining. It sounds as though the storm's moved away."

I didn't know where to start. I knew it was going to be extremely difficult to convince Isobel about the Tree-Spirits and the evil Shadow Thief. But I had no choice. I needed her help, even though she was a girl.

"Isobel, please button it will you? It's not going to be easy for you to take it all in, but please give me a chance to explain my odd behaviour. Oh, just hold on a minute will you. I need to collect my duffel bag from outside, there's something very important inside you must see."

It didn't take me long to nip outside and return to the kitchen clutching my trusty duffel bag close to my chest, all the while scanning with my beady eyes around the garden. All seemed calm out there for the time being.

I assumed my unusual band of friends would be cowering inside the bag. Also, I hadn't the foggiest idea how Isobel would react when she came face-to-face with them. Let's hope she doesn't do a girly thing and scream the house down.

"So. Come on then, let's hear what you have to say" she said sarcastically, shuffling around in her chair and clicking her tongue. This was another annoying habit she had; girls!

"Okay, here goes." My fingers were tightly crossed. Sweat was beginning to bead on my brow. I mopped it up with the palm of my hand, wiping it down my trouser leg.

Certain I had Isobel's undivided attention, I rested my elbows on the table and began my unbelievable story from when I bought the Tree-Spirits from the weird white-haired old man at the stall in the fair ...

After fifteen nervous and fidgety minutes, during which time Isobel was constantly staring into space, her mouth wide open, catching flies, I carefully eased my duffel bag up from the floor onto my knees, unzipping it. I then indicated with a wave of my hand for Isobel to come over and take a look inside.

"Please, please don't scream out loud as you will only frighten them; also, I don't want your Mum and Dad to know what we are getting up to."

"Barnaby, I'm warning you. If there's a snake or something else nasty hiding in there which is going to jump out and attack me. I will throttle you and give you one of my famous Indian burns. Do you understand?"

I nodded as I slowly eased open the top of the duffel bag for Isobel to peer inside. I then waited with bated breath for her reaction.

"Oh my God, Barnaby," she gasped, putting her hands up to her mouth, at the same time jumping off her chair as though someone had pinched her bottom. "What on earth are they? Are they real or are they some kind of new fandangle American toys your Dad bought on one of his overseas trips?"

Looking up from the gloomy surroundings of the bottom of the duffel bag, four pairs of bleary eyes stared back up at us.

"Barnaby, where have you been? And next time don't leave us outside in the cold on our own again. And did you hear that thunder a few minutes ago? Well, it wasn't your normal thunder. It was Nanny Buttoncap celebrating. That means *she* must have Aticuss and Fay. Please tell me I'm wrong Barnaby, and once again you've forgotten our password. You have to be more careful in future?" said Figment, adjusting his eyes from the glare of the overhead fluorescent light. I whispered "Sorry," with the feeling as though I'd let him down, forgetting our password. Also, I didn't have the heart to tell the four of them that someone resembling my Dad had taken the Tree-Spirits. It didn't matter anyway, because I was pretty sure they all knew by the worried expression on my face.

"Please help us out of this smelly bag will you, Barnaby, it's now becoming a bit cramped in here for the four of us," came the frail voice of Figment.

One at a time I gingerly placed the four figures on top of the kitchen table, leaving Isobel to stare over at them in utter amazement. Her mouth was wide open. She was totally speechless, which for the time being was probably for the best, and I don't think she'd heard Figment raise the issue about our silly password.

I quickly began to explain to the four of them about my Dad coming over to collect the Tree-Spirits, and why it couldn't have been him as he was fast asleep in our house when we'd left. Rosie Apple broke down in tears, resting her head on Tickety-Boo's shoulder for comfort. As all this was going on, Knuckledown stumbled across the kitchen table on his wobbly stick legs, falling down a couple of times. Feeling sorry for the little man, I gingerly picked him up, cautiously resting him on the palm of my sweaty hand.

Once settled, ensuring the points of his legs weren't sticking into my skin, he glanced up into my eyes before speaking.

"Barnaby, please don't blame yourself. Nanny Buttoncap can't have gone very far, now can she? And if she's in the guise of your Dad, we may be able to find her if we get a move on. So, instead of all feeling sorry for ourselves, let's get out there and start searching for her, him, or whatever you want to call it."

There was a moment of subdued silence as we all tried to accept that Aticuss and Fay were now in the hands of Nanny Buttoncap. Surprisingly, it was Isobel who eventually brought us out of our musing.

"This is my entire fault, Barnaby," whimpered Isobel, "And if I hadn't been so stupid and childish taking the two Tree-Spirits from your tree, this wouldn't have happened. So if it's fine with you lot, I'd like to tag along and help you find the Tree-Spirits. It's the least I can do. And please keep your voice down. I don't want Mum and Dad to come down to investigate the noise we've been making. Especially after this morning's encounter with your Dad, or whatever you say it was. My parents aren't too well pleased with your family, and I can assure you they aren't the flavour of the month at this moment."

My mind was a blur and I couldn't think straight. Was it right for Isobel to get involved and come along with me?

But where do I start searching? It could be anywhere by now.

Once again it was Isobel's constant ranting that eventually brought me out of my daydream.

" ... And Barnaby, I'll need to take some warm clothes as we don't know how long we'll be out there searching for them," she said, trying hard to keep her voice under control.

By this time my little group of weird-looking friends had gathered together for some comfort and support as they were now relying on two humans who had no experience at all in finding magical, horrible Shadow Thieves. Thankfully, Figment finally agreed it would be a good idea to try and find my Dad, or whoever it was, especially it being daylight and all. He also said he couldn't imagine Nanny doing anything out of the ordinary as it would only attract undue attention. I also wondered why he wasn't suggesting doing anything to help us out. Why was he leaving it to us two mortals?

"Come on then Isobel, grab your shoes and coat while I get these four settled. We *must* find Aticuss and Fay before Twelfth Night," I stated, carefully placing the four of them at the bottom of the now smelly duffel bag.

Some five minutes later we were outside in the cold, yet the warmth from the sun was just strong enough to warm my freezing-cold face. In the meantime, Isobel had gone to collect her bike from the garden shed.

As we were slowly making our way out of the back garden, hundreds of weird thoughts began to go round and round my confused mind, not knowing what was in store for us ...

We'd only cycled a few minutes when we came upon my noisy next-door neighbour, Mr. Croad.

"You're up bright and early Barnaby, couldn't you sleep? And I've just seen your Dad down the road, chatting to some of the gypsies who are helping out at the circus that's in town. If you're lucky, you may be able to catch him up. Happy New Year to you both, and I like your new bike. Christmas present?"

"Yes it is, and a happy new year to you and Mrs. Croad," I called back.

Satisfied the duffel bag was firmly strapped to my back, I indicated with a sweep of my hand for Isobel to lead the way.

"Did you hear what Mr. Croad said? Dad's down here somewhere. Hold on tight, I'm going to be riding hard?" I shouted over my shoulder at the duffel bag. If anyone had been watching me, they would have thought I'd lost my mind. But then again ... I may have!

"I don't know about you, but when I think of gypsies, I instantly see visions of horse-drawn wagons, little old ladies doing a bit of fortune-telling wearing brightly-coloured scarves covering their heads with hairy warts dotted all over their faces, knocking on doors trying to sell carved wooden clothes pegs from bags made out of odd pieces of brightly-coloured carpet. I've been told they can turn their hand to most things to make a living.

"As for the men, well, they always look scruffy to me, with their long dirty tangled hair and unwashed beards and rounded pieces of metal similar to curtain hooks stuck in their ears. (In 1967, earrings weren't as fashionable as they are today.)

"The men would go out at night in groups, prowling the streets, searching for the next child to steal. I know, I know, my mind's working overtime as usual. But

when you are young and innocent, that's what parents
tended to tell their children to ensure they were good
and not getting into any kind of mischief ..."

Minutes later, as we were rounding a corner, I thought I spotted Dad entering a newsagent's just a few yards away. Isobel had also spied him.

"You wait outside while I pop inside to check if it is Dad or not. And can you keep hold of the duffel bag for safe keeping, just in case it is my Dad and not Nanny? He may start asking some awkward questions about what I've got hidden inside," I said, checking to see if anyone was leaving the shop.

Carefully easing the duffel bag from around my arms and shoulders, I handed it over to a nervous-looking Isobel.

"Don't worry, Isobel, if it's Nanny Buttoncap, I don't think she will do anything stupid in there as I can see a few customers wandering around by the stacked shelves of magazines," I said, trying to convince myself.

"Good luck, Barnaby, and don't do anything brave or stupid in there, will you?" whispered Isobel, as I eased the door open with the jangling of tinny bells above my head.

"As if I would be brave. I'm not that blooming daft, or daring!" I thought, trembling with fear.

Entering the shop, the tinkling of the brass bell echoed around the small confines of the shop and the paper dust, combined with the smell of fresh ink from the newly printed morning newspapers, tickled my cold, runny nose.

Chapter Eight

Shuffling nervously toward the sweet counter, I sneaked a glance around the cramped shop, searching for Dad. There were only six customers nosing around the shelves where the magazines were lined up and none of them resembled Dad in the slightest. I must have been mistaken, and he hadn't entered the shop in the first place. Or has Nanny Buttoncap changed once again, yet I can't imagine she would have done that, especially inside a busy shop?

"Hi Barnaby, you're up bright and early. Have you come to collect your Dad's fishing magazine?" asked the shopkeeper as he carried on sorting through the piles of morning newspapers on the counter. I couldn't help but notice that the tips of his fingers were covered in black ink. I wouldn't fancy sifting through newly-printed newspapers every morning!

It was then that I came to the conclusion that it couldn't have been Dad who'd entered the newsagent's in the first place. "Must have been mistaken, thank goodness?" I thought, releasing a pent-up breath I'd been holding.

"No thanks, he said he'll be collecting it some time this afternoon. I've just popped in for some sweets," I replied, pushing my way to the front of the queue, in the process colliding with an old woman who was waiting patiently to be served. After hastily paying for a tube of Smarties I apologised to the angry-looking woman and bolted out of the shop.

"Well, was your Dad in there, or was it that Nanny

What's-her-name?" asked an impatient Isobel, easing her bike away from the newsagent's wall, at the same time handing over the duffel bag with her trembling fingers as though it was about to explode in her hands.

"Nope. The shopkeeper asked me if I was calling in to collect Dad's magazine. The rest of customers seemed to be normal, as old people go anyway. Come on Isobel, let's go and find these travelling gypsies ..." I suddenly stopped mid-sentence, because pasted on the wall directly next to me was a brightly-coloured four-foot poster advertising the circus listing all the towns and villages they were to perform in. To my sheer horror their venue for the next three days was to be on the common just outside Skipton on the cold, windy Yorkshire Moors. You see, I remembered Figment mentioning to me about 'The Unseelie Court' who appear in groups at night and harass humans by taking them up into the air, or leading them astray "and they lived mostly on the wild and windy moors".

I was pretty certain that was where Nanny Buttoncap was heading. No doubt she will be trying to be close to her weird and hideous friends until Twelfth Night, and also be on the look-out for more unsuspecting children who may have recently bought some Tree-Spirits.

I chose not to tell Figment and the others where we were going for the time being. I'd tell them when we got closer to the moors. There's no point in worrying them, not just yet anyway, but it did make me shiver to think what would happen to me and my family if I didn't find some way of getting the Tree-Spirits safely back home in time.

Then, much to my utter annoyance and complete surprise, Isobel informed me that she'd had enough and was in the process of wheeling her bike in the opposite direction to where I was heading.

"Barnaby, I've had enough of this chasing around for some silly weird Tree- Spirits, so I'm setting off back home. You can go and find your stupid friends by yourself. But don't worry; I won't say anything to anyone about what happened this morning. And to be honest with you, I don't think they would believe me if I told them. See you later and good luck."

"You, not say anything? No way."

"I won't," she replied, nodding.

"Cross your heart and hope to die?"

She drew an invisible X over her heart with her index finger. "Promise," she said.

"Yeah, and pigs can fly. Please don't go Isobel," I pleaded. "I'm going to need all the help I can get, even though you're a girl. Sorry, I didn't mean that." I could have kicked myself for saying that, even though the thought did cross my mind.

"Not after that petty remark I'm not. You can clear off. You're on your own now little boy," she called out, pedalling away down the road, shaking her head and clicking her tongue.

"Please Isobel, I'm sorry," I yelled at the top of my voice.

"Bye Barnaby," she called back over her shoulder.

With a heavy heart I stood frozen to the spot, staring at the diminishing figure of Isobel, feeling totally abandoned and lonely.

I knew there was no point in feeling sorry for myself, so I rested the bike up against my leg before checking inside the duffel bag. Certain that the four of them were nicely settled I headed off to where the gypsy camp was located. I didn't have the heart to tell them we were now on our own.

"Oh dear, oh dear, what have I got myself into now?" I muttered under my breath. I had a bad feeling about all of this.

Some fifteen agonising minutes later I arrived by the wasteland where the gypsy caravans had been set up.

To my disappointment, the muddy field was completely deserted apart from the dozens of bulging black bin bags jam-packed with festering rubbish, along with an odd assortment of broken furniture that had been dumped in the centre of the field. The distinctive smell of horse manure and rotting food drifted around in the cold morning air. I sneezed a couple of times from the horrible stench and my eyes began to sting.

There was one consolation, though. I knew the gypsies couldn't have gone too far because of the small traces of fires that had been left to burn out that were dotted around the field. And, as luck would have it, apart from the numerous snaking tracks on the road left by the muddy wooden wheels of the caravans, there was also dozens of hoof prints from the horses that pulled the caravans, leaving a nice line down the road, thank you very much. As long as the mud lasted on the road, I should be able to follow them to their next port of call – the moors. "UGH!"

Now that I was in a position where I wanted some kind of help and support, I carefully unzipped the duffel bag, informing them of my intentions.

"Right, guys and gals, it's going to get a bit bumpy over the next thirty minutes or so and you're going to be cooped up in there for a little while longer, so make yourself as comfortable as possible. I'm heading off towards the moors. I'm pretty certain that's were Nanny Buttoncap is going, along with a group of gypsies to keep her company."

"Barnaby," whispered Figment. "Please sit down for a while and listen to what I have to say. I want to discuss something very important with you."

Suddenly I became interested in what Figment had to say, so I did I was told, slumping down heavily onto a graffiti-covered bench positioned a few yards from the wasteland. "Come on then, what's so important it can't wait?" I asked impatiently.

Raising his worried body, Figment began to tell me what was on his mind.

"Barnaby, you may have noticed that your Christmas decorations, Rosie Apple and Bright Eyes, have now fully-grown wings. And after a long and meaningful discussion, they have both volunteered to fly off in search of Aticuss and Fay. Don't be alarmed; they won't come to any harm, I can assure you. They will certainly know what to do in a crisis. And I have instructed them to get word back to me, if and when they do find the Tree-Spirits."

What could I say? If they did find Aticuss and Fay, everything would be back to normal, I wished.

After a moment of tense, nervous silence there was a blast from inside the bag, followed by Bright Eyes and Rosie Apple sailing gracefully out of the yawning mouth, leaving a trail of crimson sparkles in their wake along with a pulsating sphere of brilliant white light, together with a multicoloured nucleus circling over them. Their flowing golden hair, together with their dazzling opulent outspread wings combined to make a brilliant ever-changing hue that appeared just seconds before they took flight into the early morning air.

I stood there with my mouth open, witnessing the unbelievable scene in front of me, also trying to hold down a lump that was forming in my throat, knowing my hand-made decorations were only trying to help me out. Then out of the blue, two loud explosions, similar to firecrackers, went off high above us. Then, in a flash, the two beautiful creatures left a dazzling streak of purple light across the sky, and disappeared in the blink of an eye. Not even a distant speck was left on the horizon.

After that moment of wonderment Figment then surprisingly informed me that he was also going to take his leave and he would be taking Knuckledown with him.

"Barnaby, please accept my sincere apologies. But I had to be certain where Aticuss and Fay were being taken before deciding to search for them. And you were correct all along. I do have the power to transform the appearance of others and myself. I can also control my stature and size. But not here, it's far too dangerous. So my friend, I bid you farewell and a safe journey, and I hope to meet up with you at some time in the future. In the meantime, I will still need your help in finding Aticuss and Fay, as it won't be easy. Nanny Buttoncap is the most powerful faerie that has ever set foot in your world. So be wary of strangers you may bump into on the moors, as you never know who you are talking too ... Oh, and before I forget, please pop these four leaf clovers safely inside your pocket. I don't know if you are aware, but four leaf clovers can help break spells from any nasty faeries you may run into. You only need to stroke the leaves gently to make them work. You never know Barnaby, they may come in handy at some point in the future."

I swallowed and cleared my throat. "Thanks," I said, somewhat confused, slipping the bunch of four leaf clovers in my coat pocket for safekeeping. I just sat there shaking my head. I was completely lost for words. He'd been toying with me all along and I'd fallen for it. I wanted to kick myself. Somewhere out there on the moors was a village I'd deprived of its idiot. I'd been set up and he'd had taken me for a complete fool. He had intended all along to seek out Aticuss and Fay. Yet he could have taken his leave at any time during the night or even this morning. Anyway, I wasn't going to question him about that, and he did say he had to be sure where Aticuss and Fay were heading. The main thing was that he admitted that he had the powers to change shape, and moreover, he may find the way to seek out the Tree-Spirits, which was some small consolation in trying to get my life back to some semblance of order.

"Barnaby, just think clearly for a second about what I'm about to say before you judge me. Can you imagine the hundreds of awkward questions thrown at you if we were seen together? How would you have behaved, and more to the point, how would the ones asking the questions react? It certainly would have put you in an unimaginable situation. So, in the meantime, thank you for all your help and please take care of yourself, and not to worry, I won't desert you."

I was lost for words.

In a flash an overpowering nimbus of ambient blue light surrounded Figment and Knuckledown before darting off skywards, leaving behind a visible shimmer of blue, dust like motes, just inches from my upraised face. There was a glitter of silver light around them and a popping sound that made me blink. When I opened my eyes again, they were gone. I immediately felt a hidden energy swirling and rushing around my body, knocking me off balance.

The hairs at the nape of my neck prickled and stood on end. I didn't move a solitary inch. I just stood there, shivering from the cold, chewing on my bottom lip for a second, trying to think.

I must have sat there for some time, wondering what to do, because once again darkness fell around me and the wind suddenly sprung up, causing the wet leaves and soggy newspapers to chase each other around my feet; some of them even ended up being caught up in the spokes of the wheels of my bike. Then an enormous loud rumble of thunder could be heard in the distance. By now the dark clouds were becoming thicker and the rain started once more in force.

Yet there was some small amount of relief about all of this. From now on, I had only myself to worry about.

Rain fell in sheets rather than drops, sluicing down into my eyes. My hair was slowly being plastered to my head by the rain. I wiped my brow, sweeping water away, only to have it fill my vision once again. Glancing down at the gutters, I spotted the filthy rainwater collecting and coursing into the already overflowing blocked drains. The whistling of the wind sang in my ears, ruffling my hair. The rain was so heavy I had to squint to see into the distance, and within seconds my clothes and hair were soaking wet. I began to shiver from the cold and damp, a wave of exhaustion and dizziness swept over me. I was also frightened, wondering what was in store for me. . ?

"I'm sorry reader, but I need to take another short break. My fingers are beginning to cramp up from all this writing. Also, I have to collect my gear from the back room and move away from here in the next couple of hours. Hopefully I may find someplace safer and

much more comfortable. The dilemma I have is that I can only stay in one place for a couple of days at a time. If I stay any longer, I know that ... shush, stay calm and don't move a muscle. I'll get back to you as soon as I can. There's someone or something lurking just inches from the door ...

Chapter Nine

"Jeez ... that was a close call. Anyway, don't you concern yourself about me, I'm fine now thanks.

"Over time, you eventually get used to the weird antics of that lot out there and the hostile world I've found myself caught up in. Still, this place seems to be safe enough for the time being.

"While I think of it, I'll let you into a little secret of mine. But you have to promise me that you won't breathe a word of it to anyone, not even your parents ... promise? ... Good.

"I can always tell when 'they' are close by, due to the revolting odour that emanates from their clothes and bodies. Please don't laugh, but they smell of rotting fish and sweaty socks ... Ugh!

"Now where were we before we were rudely interrupted? Oh yes, I remember now, it had started to rain once more, and my hair and clothes were dripping wet ..."

Feeling thoroughly downhearted, wet and utterly miserable, I wheeled my bike over to an overhanging oak tree for some welcoming shelter, hoping the rain would soon stop. The air felt much cooler beneath the tree, and it also gave me a small amount of protection from the driving rain. And to my joy, I could hear the sound of birds calling in the trees far, far away, which lifted my spirits slightly.

After thirty minutes the storm finally died down, moving away to the east. The flashes of lightning were more distant, and the gaps between these and the subsequent rumbles of thunder grew. Eventually the rain stopped, replaced by the sun breaking through the wispy clouds giving off a warm feeling all over my dripping wet face and damp clothes.

Once I'd shaken the rain droplets from my damp jacket and wiped away the moisture from my face and hair with my bloodied handkerchief, I mounted my bike and carefully followed the muddy tracks down the road, churning up twigs and debris on the way, all the time aware it would lead me to the wild and windy moors. My heart was racing, my stomach clenched, and my skin felt clammy at the thought of what could happen if the nasty Shadow Thief caught me? With that dreadful thought in mind, I knew I had to be alert at all times and keep calm.

The constant rain had made the roads dangerous, and it was difficult trying to follow the muddy tracks on the partly submerged road, at the same time looking where I was going. On a number of occasions irate drivers honked their horns, before hastily swerving to one side, trying to avoid knocking me off my bike. It was at that traumatic point of my journey when I thought it would be wise to rest a while and have something to eat. By this time I was both hungry and jaded.

Freewheeling my bike into an empty bus shelter, I gently laid the duffel bag on the damp littered ground before unzipping it with my cold, clumsy fingers, pulling out one of the bottles of pop along with the bickies.

Minutes later, feeling refreshed, I carefully slipped my empty bottle of pop and what was left of my biscuits back into the duffel bag before setting off down the road, hopefully in the right direction towards where the gypsies were heading.

It was hard going at first; my whole body was soon bathed in sweat. But to my relief, the next thirty minutes was uneventful.

Eventually, I reached the start of the wild unfamiliar moors that looked both ugly and flat, and also menacing.

The light was now slowly fading, and in the distance I could see a dense forest that carpeted the whole landscape. There was also a light dusting of snow covering a wide area, and a fine mist began to shift across the heather just a few feet in front of me.

Feeling tired I sat down and leaned against the wall, pillowing my head in my hand, hoping to get my breath back and sheltering from the cold wind which had suddenly sprung up.

I wasn't as fit as I thought. I was totally exhausted, wet and feeling lonely ...

Lifting my weary body up from the soggy floor on my wobbly legs, I began to survey the scene in front of me. After adjusting my eyes to the gloomy surroundings, I noticed a faint light glowing on the horizon; a bonfire perhaps, or could it be the circus and, more importantly, the gypsies?

Climbing on the now wet and muddy seat of my bike, the air misted in front of me as I took a few deep breaths. My stomach was knotting up, as I wondered if I was doing the right thing. I didn't stop to consider my options, I carried on regardless.

The further I pedalled towards the light, the darker the sky became. The wind continued to rise, and overhead the clouds began to blot out the stars.

By now the moors were shrouded in a fine damp mist that clung to my hair and clothes. Thunder rumbled once more, and the ground shook beneath my feet. Lightning flashed along with it, and the ground all around me lit with a sudden azure fire that slowly faded away.

It was then when I decided to stop and listen for anyone or anything in the vicinity. Nothing. Except for my laboured breathing, there was an eerie silence all around me.

Then, from the corner of my eye, I could have sworn I saw a fleeting glimpse of a shadow moving by the other side of a wall just a few yards over to my right. My mouth gaped opened with fear, and I began to shiver with fright. Then an odd feeling crept over me, and the hairs on my neck stood up. Someone was watching me. I looked around. There was no one in sight. Was I alone?

"I've got a nasty feeling about all of this," I wheezed, pushing myself onwards.

The road was littered with dozens of deep potholes, all filled with murky rainwater. I tried very hard to avoid them, at the same time searching for the mysterious shadowy figure. But at the moment there was no one in sight – thank goodness.

When I felt I was a safe distance from the fires, I climbed off my bike and chose a secluded spot by the side of the wall; slowly crouching down, as I didn't want to be spotted, especially if Nanny Buttoncap was in the area. Then I had a horrible thought. I'd forgotten about those frightening creatures I'd spotted at the fair, and more importantly, The Unseelie Court. Could they have been what I saw on the other side of the wall? I was now petrified, so I quickly searched around on the muddy floor for some kind of a weapon. Nothing. The only thing I had was my trusty penknife that was stuffed down the inside of my jeans pocket. But I couldn't imagine that being any good against Nanny and her friends.

Cautiously easing myself up off the muddy ground, I tentatively sneaked a glance over the top of the wall.

My eyes swept over the gloomy scene before me. Some hundred yards away, I could see a sprinkling of orange campfires through the sparse-looking trees, and amongst the curling tongues of flames I could just make out the outlines of several dozen bodies sitting cross-legged near the centre of the camp.

In contrast, the field next door was alive with activity. Under the glare of a number of large powerful lights there were dozens of gypsies, halfway through erecting the circus tent. I was instantly fascinated by the hustle and bustle, not realising how many people it took to erect a circus tent. People were rushing around like ants. It was a huge operation, but they all moved like clockwork, knowing their place and what was expected of them. I was mesmerised, for what felt like hours, by the comings and goings. It was an impressive sight when it was finally finished. It was tall, round and red, and decorated all over with the pictures of the performers.

Then, to my utter alarm, I thought I detected a vaguely human shape materialising out of the mist. Perhaps shapes, plural. Something's there, someone's heading my way. A chill shot up my back, my breath caught in my throat and my stomach dropped about five feet. "Gulp!"

An outline gradually became more distinct through the mist, as if drawing closer and closer to me. Emerging from the swirling fog was a dark and menacing silhouette. It resembled a huge gorilla that grew larger and more terrifying with each long stride. In a flash I lowered myself to the dirt-covered ground. I couldn't be sure if the figure had seen me, so I began to crawl on my stomach toward the wall, carefully laying my bike down on the muddy ground.

Suddenly the wind began to howl, and over the noise I heard approaching voices combined with the scraping sound of heavy footfalls coming my way. My heart was pounding like a jackhammer in my chest and my mouth had become dry. I should be getting used to this by now, don't you think?

In order not to be seen by whoever was heading my way, I crouched down as low as possible, quietly shuffling my way closer toward the side of the wall. As all this was going on, the pain in the back of my hand intensified as the noise gradually increased. I tried to ignore the pain, and the nervous tension in my stomach made me want to throw up.

Slowly, the footfalls became louder and nearer to my hiding place. I held my breath when the footsteps approached me. They came within ten feet, then five. I felt the air stir when it walked past me no more than a foot away, making the leaves brush up against the side of my face. Then to my sheer horror, the footfalls abruptly stopped. A shiver ran though my whole body.

I swallowed the sickly taste of fear. I then clenched my teeth, slowly lifting my head, twisting it slightly to one side. A few inches from my bug eyes was a pair of black, muddy combat boots. Then the shadow bent down towards the side of my cold damp face, sending another shiver through my body. Sour breath hissed against my cold cheek. I was sickened by the stench of decay. Then in a flash, I felt light-headed and my vision began to blur. I felt a breeze brush my face, a sense of movement, but I couldn't have said whether I was falling or rising or moving forward. Then I was plunging into an inky darkness. I felt myself being pulled through the air at a rate of knots ...

Chapter Ten

The movement stopped and the whirling sensations passed ...

A harsh cry sounded out, my eyelashes fluttered open and, ever so slowly, the world came back into focus. It was then that I realised I had cried out. Raising my head a little I noticed that I was lying on top of a large bed inside what I could only presume was one of the gypsy caravans. I lay still for a minute, trying to clear my head.

The air smelled like a mixture of stale tobacco, body sweat and greasy food. Examining the cramped room, I noticed that it had only one window. It was partly open, and covered by a grubby curtain that wafted about in the gentle breeze. Stood up against one wall was a table cluttered with pots and greasy looking pans. Two worn out leather armchairs were positioned on either side of a wooden crate that acted as a coffee table. There was also a wood-burning stove in the centre of the room, which to my relief was giving off some welcoming warmth to my damp, chilled body.

Tentatively easing myself up from the bed, I gingerly made my way towards the open window, supporting my weight on the back of the chairs with my trembling hands. I felt both unsteady and dazed. My head hurt.

I cautiously parted the curtains, cupping my hands against the window, peering out into the night. I couldn't see too much due to the dirt and grime that was coating the outside of the window. My cold breath misted up the windowpane; I hastily cleared it away with my coat sleeve. Slap-bang in front of me were dozens of caravans set round in a wide circle. Small tents had also been erected in the centre close to the campfires. All the caravans were decked with hundreds of brightly coloured lights which were strung around the edges of the roof, covering all sides. The dazzling effect reminded me of Santa's grotto I'd visited at the big department store in town when I was just five. The hundreds of bright lights were throwing out a cocktail of colours on the dirt-encrusted ground and blanketing the dozens of tents along with the people wandering around the area. The sight was magical, and it took my breath away.

People were everywhere; women doing chores, men hanging around chatting and smoking, and children running around the campfires. From this distance the children looked unwashed and grubby. And I couldn't help but notice that most of the men had long straggly greasy hair. Some of them had ponytails!

Then my breath caught in my mouth. I stood rooted to the spot as my eyes focused on some of the faces of the people who were wandering around the campsite. Just a few feet from me was an assortment of strange folk and even stranger creatures all jabbering to one another? Then to my disgust I noticed one of them biting into a chunk of meat that had long strips of stringy gristle, all dripping with blood. My stomach was doing somersaults, and my heart lurched into my mouth. I'll tell you this reader; it took all of my willpower not to be sick on the floor of the caravan.

"Barnaby, what have you got yourself into?" I cried out, burying my face in the smelly curtain.

I hastily began to search around the caravan for some

kind of weapon. The floor was littered with wooden toys and dolls alongside dirty clothes and strips of coloured material; odd-shaped trunks and boxes were positioned down the sides. But I knew deep down that whatever I found would be utterly useless after seeing those revolting creatures roaming around the campsite.

I sank to the littered floor on my hands and knees, crying. My whole body was shaking with the thought of what may be in store for me...

Chapter Eleven

It was the creaking of the caravan door, combined with the flickering orange glow of the campfires through the partly-open doorway that brought me out of my sorry state of mind. I lifted my head and opened my eyes a tad, only to see a fearsome looking creature blocking my escape route. Nanny Buttoncap I presumed! My heart leapt into my throat. My first instinct was to run. But deep down, I knew I had no chance of getting past her.

The creature must have been at least eight feet tall, and it moved toward me with a liquid grace. Also to my horror, there was NO evidence of a shadow coming from the figure!

"This I definitely don't need at my time of life," I thought, despairingly.

Scared out of my skin, I quickly scampered away from IT, retreating until my back was up against the foot of the bed. I had to find some way of getting out of here, FAST!

The shadow's feet pounded in rapid succession as it headed my way. And the floor of the caravan shook as it grew closer and closer to me.

I hesitated for a split second, and then, without a thought for my welfare, I pushed myself to a sitting position, before springing to my feet, lashing out with my right boot toward the shadow. To my joy, my boot connected with the side of its head, knocking it sideways to the cluttered floor. IT cried out in surprise and gracefully floated back to its feet, once again blocking my path to the door. I then threw myself at it with all my strength, screaming wildly. But IT was too quick for me, and it was soon way out of reach. Its movements resembled a black spectre.

Before I knew it, IT punched me in the stomach, knocking the breath from my lungs. I collapsed heavily onto my knees, biting my tongue, leaving a metallic taste in my mouth. I was stunned, my ears were ringing; stars and cartoon birdies danced in my vision. I rolled to one side, trying to get away before IT could strike again.

The shadow slowly turned its head towards me, sucking in a deep long breath and then threw back its head. A long falsetto-pitched scream, similar to a demented hyena, spilled out of ITs mouth, resulting in the whole caravan shaking as though it was in a tropical storm. The many objects in the caravan began to shake, rattle and roll before exploding into small pieces that rained down to the already-littered floor. The vibrations felt like shock waves that hammered my whole body. It was at that awful stage that I knew I was in some deep serious trouble.

Taking a deep breath, preparing myself for the worse, I slyly slipped my shaky hand inside my back pocket of my jeans, fumbling around for the small bundle of four leaf clovers. I held my nerve as I gently fingered them in my pocket. Once they were safely gripped in my trembling fingers, I began to slowly caress the leaves. Then, to my alarm, the back of my hand felt as though someone was sticking red-hot needles into my skin. But once I'd got over the initial shock of the pain, I sat there stroking the clover, waiting in sheer terror to see what she had in mind: something nasty no doubt after my attack on her.

As soon as the dozens of rattling objects around the caravan had stopped shaking the shadow gradually hovered across the cluttered room, towards me, all the while making a quiet wheezing sound that might have been a laugh.

Time seemed to slow down. Then the moment was gone; slow motion to normal speed. Once again, everything went black, and within seconds I had the horrible sensation of dropping like a stone down a long dark chasm, the cold wind whipping past my face. Darkness swallowed me, and kept me there for a long time. There was nothing but silence ...

Chapter Twelve

"Barnaby, Barnaby, please will you wake up? You're starting to frighten me, now. Can you hear me?" came the distant muffled voice that was piercing my fog-filled brain.

Slowly, and somewhat cautiously, I eased my eyes open, only to see to my amazement and sheer joy Isobel's terror-stricken face glaring down at me!

"Isobel, please be careful, Nanny Buttoncap's nearby. Hide. I don't want her to catch you as well," I cried out, quickly glancing over her shoulder for any unwelcome guests and noticing I was sprawled out on my back by the side of the wall with my mud stained bike lying close by.

"What on earth are you talking about Barnaby? There's nobody here apart from us two. You haven't gone and fallen off your bike and banged your head have you, nutcase?"

In a flash I was on my feet scanning the area around me for Nanny or any other nasty blood-curdling beasts for that matter. To my relief there was no evidence of anyone about, apart from Isobel who looked to be in a state of shock. Weird or what? Then I remembered the clover. "Those weird-looking plants must have broken the spell, or have I have been hallucinating, or could it be the thorn digging its way into my hand that's making me have these weird dreams? Yet it felt so real?" I thought.

"Jeez, thank goodness for that. It was only a nasty faerie spell ... anyway, what made you decide to come and find me? Did your guilty conscience get the better of you?" I snapped, shaking with fear from the awful nightmare.

"No it didn't, so there, smarty pants. I began to worry about you being out here all by yourself on the moors. So there was no way I was going to leave you searching for that Nanny Bellybutton thing," she replied with some venom, biting her bottom lip.

"Buttoncap!"

"Whatever. Anyway, what's that old saying? Two heads are better than one when it comes to sorting things out ... shush, just be quiet for a second will you, I thought I heard the sounds of people singing somewhere out there on the moors. Do you think it may be those gypsies, Barnaby?"

I didn't answer her straight away, because I was still spooked from the horrible dream, also the back of my hand was beginning to tingle.

"If you look carefully over to your right Isobel, you may be able to see in the distance small pinpricks of light coming from dozens of camp fires. And yes, it is the gypsies ... the duffel bag?" I cried out, frantically searching the muddy floor.

"Phew, found it. Thank goodness for that." Letting out a long sigh, I then suddenly remembered the four of them leaving me to fend for myself a short while ago.

"Oh, by the way Isobel, Rosie Apple and Tickety-Boo have gone searching for the Tree-Spirits; also Figment and Knuckledown decided to leave me on my own. And you may be interested to know that Figment informed me that he was a very powerful and important faerie, and he is aiming to find Aticuss and Fay with his magical powers. So it looks as though we are on our own for the time being. Are you still up for it? It could be a little bit dangerous out there you know."

"Yeah," she said. "It isn't every day you come up against weird and terrifying faeries, is it?" she added, sidling over beside me, grabbing hold of my sweaty hand for protection, and some comfort.

"What have you done to your hand, Barnaby? You need to put some ointment on that as soon as you can. It looks really sore, is it?" she asked caringly.

"Oh that. It's nothing. I grazed it on one of the thick prickly branches on the Christmas tree when I was helping Dad the other night. And did you notice, we had one of those Scandinavian trees this year," I replied, attempting to change the subject.

"It doesn't look good. Have you had anyone look at it?" she asked with concern in her voice.

I shook my head. "No time," I lied.

I tried to take her mind off my wounded hand by draping a protective arm around her shoulder.

Isobel shrugged her shoulders and we said nothing more on the matter, for now.

We stood side by side in silence for a while, glancing up into the night sky. It was crystal clear, and the light from the moon was casting an ethereal glow around the uninviting dismal-looking moors that spread out for miles and miles before us ...

Chapter Thirteen

"Have you any thoughts about what you intend doing now, Barnaby?" enquired Isobel, gazing into my eyes.

"I don't think we have any alternative but to check out the gypsy camp for the Tree-Spirits, and what we do when we find them is another thing altogether. We'll have to decide that when that moment arises. Are you game, or what?"

After a few minutes of going over what we intended to do, we both agreed to check out the gypsy camp for Aticuss and Fay.

Stealthily making our way toward the glowing fires of the campsite we thought it would be best to abandon our bikes due to the ground being boggy, knowing that it would be extremely difficult cycling in those conditions.

So, cautiously, we began to circle the campsite, eventually reaching an area close to a line of Hawthorne bushes that overlooked the site from a distance of about twenty feet. Luckily the bushes were dense enough for us to keep a careful watch over the gypsies without being seen.

I don't know if you are aware, but darkness can be both friend and foe; friend because it aids your concealment, foe because you can't be sure if there is anyone lurking close by.

Once we'd got our breath and composure back we slowly made our way down a well-trodden winding path, becoming ever closer to the campsite; picking our way through the dense undergrowth, stumbling around bends, tripping over large stones and dodging between boulders the size of double-decker buses.

Coming to a halt just feet from the nearest campfire, we scrambled on our hands and knees, creeping beneath an overhanging rock for shelter, hoping we wouldn't be spotted. And you should have seen the surprised expression in Isobel's eyes when she saw the breathtaking scene before us. The multitude of brightly-coloured lights adorning the caravans was out of this world. And the circus tent in the next field was huge and stunning. The only words to describe the setting before us were hair-raising, electrifying, majestic ...

By now we were both feeling at ease and somewhat overly confident that we hadn't been seen, when a large hunched, shadowy figure appeared from out of the swirling fog just a few feet in front of us moving directly towards us, its feet shuffling through the last autumn's soggy leaves. Then, to our horror, thuddy vibrations from the ground caused the trees close by to sway and shake along with dozens of stones, which rattled and slid down the hillside creating a small avalanche. I also noticed a small number of boulders shifting from their fixed position by the quake. With that in mind I scanned the area for a means of escape, spying a narrow stone passageway to my left. But it was so narrow; two people could not possibly pass through it side by side. Never mind, at least I'd found a way of getting out of this nightmare. I hoped!

Stretching over with my right hand, at the same time ensuring I was going to slip and slide down the small incline, I reached out, tapping Isobel's shoulder and motioning with a nod of my head towards the passageway, at the same time holding up my fingers to my mouth for her to keep as quiet as possible. In the meantime, the vibrations around us had abruptly stopped.

Aware that any kind of movement from either of us would give us away, I listened intently. I heard footsteps a few feet away, accompanied by the sounds of deep, guttural breathing.

Knowing we didn't have much time before the shadowy figure reached our hiding place we ducked down behind one of the boulders, cunningly making our way by sidestepping toward the passage. All I could hear now was the gurgling of a stream in the distance combined with a sniffing sound coming from far below. By the time we were mere yards from the passageway the sun had finally set, and thankfully the rain had stopped. But the ground was thick with mud, which made our progress up the steep incline painful and slow. Also the air had grown colder, and it was now becoming too dark to see where we were putting our feet.

We'd only taken a dozen steps when Isobel came to halt, holding one of her hands up for me to stop, and with the other hand pressing her fingers up to her lips for me to be silent.

I hadn't a clue what she'd seen or heard, but we waited and watched awhile, gathering our courage and holding our nerve. Some five minutes later or so we glimpsed darting movements below us. Then all of a sudden, dozens of people emerged from the trees, all walking towards us. My skin crawled, and I shivered with fright.

We both knew instinctively what to do; we ran for our lives, hoping to find the sanctuary of the cave.

Guided by the starlight, Isobel reached the opening first, and within seconds she'd disappeared into the inky darkness of the cave. A short while later I found myself by the entrance, peering into the dark void, wondering what on earth was lurking down there. Without any hesitation I clambered through the opening, glancing over my shoulder at what was happening behind me. Nothing, thank goodness. Then from out of the corner of my eye I caught a movement by the base of the hill. There wasn't just the one shadow heading our way. There were now dozens of eerie, elongated shadows, all creeping up the hill towards us! A clap of thunder broke through the silence. There was a bad storm heading our way. Forks of lightning sizzled across the sky and additional crashes of thunder tore through the night sky, loud pounding thunder! "Cripes!"

I hadn't realised, but Isobel had retraced her steps, and she was now standing right next to me, witnessing the horrible sight that was developing before us. I glanced into her eyes, only to see that she was close to tears. I moved closer and hugged her before directing her down the dark passageway with a sweep of my sweaty hand. I certainly had no intentions of waiting to see what the group of figures heading our way had on their minds.

We staggered blindly onwards down into the depths of the dark, dank cave. The metronomic sound of dripping water could be heard deep within the bowels of the earth.

In our haste, Isobel tripped on a hidden rock, landing heavily on the stone-covered ground. She picked herself up, brushed the grit from her hands down the legs of her jeans leaving a trail of dirt down the front, before carrying on without uttering a word. It was then that I knew I had someone I could rely on when the going got tough.

She's tougher than she looks, I thought, wiping away the moisture from my eyes with the tips of my fingers then carrying on into the inky darkness ...

"Hi there ... I need to rest once more, as I found it difficult trying to get to sleep last night, which to be honest with you, was no surprise to me. My head's always in a whirl with what I've seen and heard, also with the realisation of where I have found myself. You see, I've seen a multitude of scary things, and being trapped and living in this land doesn't make it any easier for me ... "

Chapter Fourteen

We'd only moved a short distance down the narrow passageway when the small amount of light coming through the opening to the cave behind us suddenly blanked out. There could only be one reason for that! The dozens of mysterious shadowy figures we'd spotted were following our tracks, blocking the light from the entrance! Let's hope that's not the only way in and out of this dark cave. If it is, we could be down here for a long, long time.

Isobel didn't need to be told what to do, in a flash she was making her way down the tunnel, all the while being extra careful where she placed her hands and feet. Meanwhile, I was carefully walking backwards using the crumbling damp lichen-covered stone walls as a means of support, checking to see whether the shadows were going to follow us or not. It was the sudden jerky movement of light at the entrance to the cave that told me they were heading our way. There was whispering and groaning in the distance and, worst of all, a faint sound of shuffling feet. Then there was silence for a while, and all I could hear was the beating of my own heart.

We pressed on further down the tunnel, going deeper underground with every nervous step; hundreds of cobwebs brushed against our faces and hair. A steady stream of water trickled by our already soaking-wet trainers. The roof of the cave was no higher than both of us, so we were not able to stand up straight as we made our way down the tunnel. The cave felt small, and the air grew colder and the light began to dim.

By the time I'd reached Isobel sweat was pouring off me, and to make matters worse, the unnerving sounds coming from behind us was getting closer by the second and growing stronger.

"Come on Isobel, we can't afford to stop and rest. They'll be on to us soon," I gasped, bending at the waist, bracing my hands on my knees.

"I can't go any further, Barnaby. I haven't got the energy. You go and find a way out of here, then come back for me. In the meantime I'll try and find somewhere safe to hide," she croaked, no doubt choking on the particles of dirt lining the back of her throat.

As we stood contemplating what to do next, we both looked back from where we'd come, only to see a curtain of air tear open, spilling out an overpowering red light. Once I'd adjusted my eyes to the sudden glare I could just make out a crimson pathway in the distance, banked on either side by a high stonewall. Then, to my surprise, the air began to shimmer in a red mist, like the heat from glowing coals on a blazing hot barbecue. Then the mist swept into the portal like a drawn breath. To our amazement appearing through the opening was Figment, bathed in a warm red glow that shone all around the walls of the tunnel.

Glancing across at us, Figment beckoned for us to step towards him, towards the bright red glowing light. I didn't know if Isobel was having the same sensation as I was, but I felt as though I was hovering just inches above the ground. My whole body started to tingle and my hair stood on end. I then began to wonder why Figment had left it until now to use his powers. Never mind I thought. If it means getting away from that lot coming our way it's fine by me, and I certainly had no intentions of questioning him at that precise moment.

After we'd passed through the glowing portal it closed behind us as suddenly as it had appeared. Figment's dark robe billowed around his feet as he stepped to one side to let us through. And I'm not entirely certain, but I think I heard the word 'Piccalilli' whispered somewhere in the dark. I grinned from ear to ear.

I've no idea how long I was floating about in mid-air, but the next thing I remembered was we were once again making our way down the winding stone passageway with Isobel leading the way.

"What was that all about, Barnaby?' she asked, jerking her head in the direction from which we'd come.

"I haven't got the foggiest idea. But as long as we are out of reach of those horrible shadowy things, I couldn't care less." I replied. I then stopped to wonder whether she was questioning me about Figment whispering 'Piccalilli', or the surprising appearance of him and the weird portal. I didn't raise the matter with her, just shook my head in bewilderment.

With our heads bent down I fell into step behind Isobel, picking up the pace as we made our way down the narrow, winding passageway.

Some minutes later the tunnel unexpectedly opened up into a large damp, high-ceilinged cavern with a rock-strewn floor. It was huge. Long dripping teeth-like stalactites hung down threateningly, their constant dripping creating milky pools of water on the floor which lapped up against our already-muddy trainers. But that wasn't the worst of it; the stench coming from the foul, milky pools was overpowering. I wrinkled my nose and quickly held my hand over my mouth to stop myself gagging. Isobel hurriedly followed suit, pulling out a lacy handkerchief from her coat pocket, covering most of her nose and mouth.

We then stood rooted to the spot, both sensing that there was something in the dark cave with us, hiding. Shapes moved around in the shadows, scurrying like rats and gliding over the dusty floor like snakes. The skin on my neck started to crawl.

Glancing up to the ceiling, I could see vague distorted outlines in the darkness, and I heard the unnerving sounds of shuffling, scraping and fluttery, irregular breathing. Or was my mind playing tricks on me again? Yet I knew it couldn't have been the thorn playing with my mind on this occasion, because I could see that Isobel was also looking frightened and somewhat agitated.

We both held our breath, dreading that whoever they were, they might have heard us. "They must be deaf if they hadn't," I thought, releasing the pent-up breath I was holding onto.

Suddenly, moving air whipped and battered our faces, causing a draft. Unfortunately, I didn't see what it was. My breath caught in my throat.

Then I nearly jumped out of my skin when Isobel screamed at the top of her lungs, the sound echoing all over the cave walls. After a few jumpy seconds, the cave was once again wrapped in silence, along with Isobel, who by now had collapsed in a heap onto the wet floor, shaking like a leaf.

"What's wrong?" I asked, straining to hear.

"We're not alone," she whispered.

Then, all of a sudden, I could hear rustling sounds all

around us, ahead, at the sides, and more worrying, high above us.

We daren't move a muscle or say a single word. And in the dim light I could see Isobel's eyes were round and wide; not with childlike wonder or excitement, but with sheer terror. I crouched down next to her, our backs pressed up against the wall for support. Isobel grasped my hand. Once again we were too scared to say a word or move. Sweat ran down my face, stinging my eyes. I began to slow down my breathing, trying my best to clear my mind. Suddenly something slithered towards me through the darkness. I stared ahead, wishing desperately that I could see more clearly.

"I've had enough of this. Are you ready?" I whispered, now panicking at the thought of what was just inches from my outstretched feet.

"Yes," she replied from out of the corner of her mouth.

Once our nerves had settled, I jerked my head to one side, indicating for Isobel to move away from here as fast as possible. She nodded her agreement, and we dashed toward a small opening in the cave wall. We had no idea where it would lead, but we didn't care. By this time my imagination was running riot as to what could have been in the cave with us, and the stench was now becoming ingrained in our hair and clothes.

We seemed to have been walking for ages, but after a while we began to slow down, before coming to a halt.

"I don't like this, Barnaby," Isobel called back, "There is a large pool of water dead ahead. And it smells bad as though something's crawled down here and died. Doesn't look safe at all ..."

The first thing that hit me was the air. It smelt disgusting. I then squeezed forward, standing by her side, glancing over her shoulder, expecting to see running water or maybe a small stream or underground river that she couldn't cross. Instead, the tunnel widened out to form a rectangular cave which contained a small lake. The water almost lapped up to the sides of the wall of the cave. To the right of us was a muddy path bordering the edge of the lake. It looked slippery and dangerous. The lake worried me. It was murky, the colour of mud, and there were ripples on the surface; something you'd expect to see on water agitated by the wind. Even as I watched, the waters stirred, moved by something out of sight beneath the surface. But we were underground, and the air was still and calm. I also had a feeling the lake was freezing cold and very deep.

"Was there something lurking under the surface?" I wondered. I didn't want Isobel to hear my thoughts. Also, the cave was eerily gloomy. There were lots of dark corners with sinister shadows. Anything or anyone could be hiding in those shadows. I slowly lifted my head up to the roof of the cave. Dozens of large crystals hung down, radiating a soft light which was just enough for us to see. As my eyes gradually became accustomed to the near darkness, I began to see movement on the floor and walls. Spiders and beetles of every shape and size were crawling up and down the walls, disappearing into the cracks and crevices as they sensed our unexpected arrival. Rats and mice the size of newborn puppies was scurrying along the floor ahead of us, and enormous droplets of water dripped into the water with an eerie plopping sound which echoed down the tunnel. I also noticed that the shadowy corners of the ceiling were covered in cobwebs, so thick and tangled that an army of spiders must have been busy at work. If only one or two

114

had spun all that, I definitely didn't want to meet them.

I started to panic, and I could feel my heart pounding in my chest. Looking more than a little nervous, Isobel, to my surprise, cautiously edged her way along the side of the cave, pausing now and again to stop from falling into the slimy water. There was no way I was going to be left behind, so I too began to make my way along the side of the cave. My heart was racing and sweat dripped into my eyes. I daren't wipe my face for fear of falling in the water; I just twisted my mouth around and blew hard, hoping to clear my eyes. It worked. Unfortunately, I hadn't warned Isobel what I was going to do, and the sudden sound of a 'raspberry' echoing around the cave nearly caused her to trip and fall. Luckily she saw the funny side and began to chuckle away to herself.

It seemed like a lifetime passed whilst trying to manoeuvre around the side of the cave, but eventually we managed to reach safety and, more importantly, dry land.

"I hope we don't come across any more of those on our travels. Next time we may not be so lucky," I gasped, bending down once again, resting my hands on my knees, trying to get my breathing back to normal.

"Come on Barnaby, we've been in this dump long enough, let's get a move on. The floor in front of us seems to be dry and clear of bricks. Are you ready to go?"

"Ready when you are, boss woman," I replied, standing to attention and saluting her.

Isobel playfully tapped me on the shoulder before heading off down the tunnel.

After ten minutes of traipsing down the low, winding passageways, rife with the smell of mould, we reached a place where the walls became rough and uneven and where shadows lay thick and heavy in the dark recesses of the cave. It was then, to our relief that we came upon some steep stone steps that had been chiselled into the wall of the cave, which disappeared into the darkness above. I also noticed to my alarm that the steps were covered in shiny, wet green algae that oozed down the walls. At that stage I knew we had to be extra careful when making our ascent. We both agreed it would be best if I took the lead. So, by using the side of the wall for some means of support, I cautiously placed my feet on the driest parts of the slimy steps, steadily climbing to where. . ? It was anybody's guess.

We'd only been climbing a few minutes when a shaft of daylight shone down from the top right-hand corner. I stopped and turned to face Isobel, smiling. Isobel returned the smile before impatiently squeezing her way past me to see what was in store for us.

Just feet from the opening we could hear the familiar loud sounds of rushing water combined with a fine watery mist that floated in the small gap, just inches from our smiling faces.

We stared at each other before scrambling the last few feet on our hands and knees and then running towards the noise, hoping it may be a safe passage out of this smelly cave.

We skidded to a halt out of the gloom, just inches from a drop of hundreds of feet, facing with what I can only describe as our escape route. We began to breathe more easily as we both felt relieved to be outside in the moonlight.

Stepping through the narrow opening we were met by an icy blast of wind and freezing cold water, finding ourselves standing on a slippery rock that jutted out from behind a large, roaring waterfall.

Before us, hundreds of gallons of cold water were tumbling and crashing down from the steep face of the cliffs, forming a large stream that sparkled from the crescent moon that danced down into a raging river in the distance. I turned slowly, taking it all in. The view was spectacular.

Both relief and joy filled my heart, knowing that we had somehow managed to escape from the caves safely. Isobel cautiously sidestepped across to be beside me, resting her head on my shivering shoulder before closing her eyes.

"I hope you're still with me, and haven't left me here all by myself. Just to get you up-to-speed, I had to quickly move from my last hiding place as I felt I was being watched by someone or something. And as luck would have it, I stumbled across a small abandoned house hidden deep in the woods. It seems to be fine for now, and it doesn't seem as though anyone's lived in here for a good while, so I may be able to rest for a few days if I'm lucky. The house is silent, aside from the occasional gusts of wind rattling the windows, but I should be used to that by now. At the moment I'm resting on a stained bare mattress in the corner of the main room, listening to the wind blowing through the trees outside. I can somehow feel the branches sway and bend with each gust of wind as I try to get my thoughts back into some semblance of order. As I mentioned to you earlier on in my narrative, my memory and concentration are not as sharp as they were. And, over the years, some of the fine details have faded away, one after another. When I'm rested, I'll once again begin to put pen to paper. But until then, please be patient with me ..."

Chapter Fifteen

Once we'd regained our composure and our breathing was back to normal Isobel dropped down to her hands and knees, pressed her back up against the moss-covered wall and bum-shuffled her way towards the far edge of the waterfall; all the while gripping the wet stones with her trembling fingers to keep from falling off into the raging river below.

At the halfway point she gingerly eased her way over a jagged fracture, freezing rushing water catching her dangling legs, threatening to pull her off. Thankfully, after an anxious few minutes, she managed to reach safety, unscathed, and seconds later she'd jumped off on the far side, wiping away the spray from her soaking wet trousers with her hands and raking her fingers through her wet straggly hair.

Certain she was safe I proceeded to follow the same route Isobel had taken. I too dropped down onto my hands and knees and bum-shuffled, letting my fingers wander, finding the cracks and handholds of the lichen-covered wall.

Before I knew it, I'd made it safely across the ledge and was gazing at the vast landscape in front of me. By now there was a bright sun high up in the sky, and it was all very picturesque. I then stopped to listen for any movement behind me. Except for my laboured breathing there was an eerie silence. By this time my imagination was beginning to run riot as I became convinced that there was somebody behind me. It still makes me shiver to think of it.

After plucking up the courage to move, I hastily spun around, only to see an empty inky blackness behind the cascading waterfall from where we'd come.

Meanwhile, Isobel had already made her way down the small incline to the foot of the waterfall, dipping her handkerchief into the cold water, washing away the grime and dirt from her hands and face. The sun's reflection off the water played against Isobel's angelic face. This caused me to feel guilty for putting her in this hazardous position in the first place. "I'll have to go down and apologise to her," I thought, feeling relived that we were out in the open once more.

Walking to the edge of the rock, I stood there for a moment, soaking up the atmosphere, listening to the thunder of the water rolling over the river and the wind stirring the water into waves nearly like those of the sea. After pulling myself together after the shock of being trapped in the caves, I steadily headed down the steep incline to the smiling face of Isobel.

On reaching her I decided to keep my mouth shut, as I knew I would only get a sarcastic reply if I started to grovel for her forgiveness. Then without any kind of warning, everything around me became a blur. I began to sway and stagger on my rubbery legs, quickly reaching out to steady myself on a large boulder to my right. Ever so slowly the world came back into focus, and in an instant my dizziness faded as quickly as it had appeared. I cautiously eased myself down onto the wet shingle for a couple of minutes to clear my head.

"What was that all about, Barnaby? You're not on any medication are you?"

"No I'm not, and I don't know what came over me just then. It was probably the stress of running around in the confines of those creepy tunnels. Anyway, thanks for your concern, I'm touched," I gasped, at the same time stroking the back of my sore hand.

"No problem. Are you ready, or do you want to rest for a few more minutes?" asked Isobel, extending her hand to help me up from the wet floor.

"I'm fine thanks, let's move away from here," I replied, easing myself up from the wet floor. I was now anxious to get away from here. Those gruesome creepy creatures following us may know another way out of these caves, and they could be silently circling us at this very minute.

Satisfied there was no one skulking about we headed off towards what we thought was the location of the gypsy campsite and, more importantly, Aticuss and Fay.

It was now beginning to brighten on the horizon, and the sky was mostly full of grey clouds blowing in from the west. In the distance I could make out the stream to the right of us curling gently towards the foot of the rocky hillside. It looked so tranquil and peaceful, and I wished my nightmare would soon come to an end – happily may I add. I also had the weirdest feeling that the landscape I saw was like nothing I'd ever seen on TV or in any of the nature books I'd taken out at the school library. The vast horizon was circled by hundreds of trees; some of them the height of skyscrapers I'd seen on the American cop shows that were currently running. I stood and paused for a moment, soaking up the wondrous scene before me. The sky was changing colours; they were all slowly merging together like a watercolour painting that had been left outside in the rain.

In the meantime, Isobel had already started to make

her way down the small incline toward the foot of the hill, totally oblivious to what was around us. It was at that point I decided to keep my feelings to myself, as I knew without a shadow of doubt that we had somehow found ourselves in Fairyland. And it was probably at some point when we walked through that portal, I guessed.

Slipping and sliding down the rocky slope we found ourselves by the banks of a river, the rushing white water churning around in torrents and splashing up against the enormous rocks and boulders that littered the riverbed.

The dreadful thought of falling into the raging water was the reason we were being extra careful, steadily manoeuvring around the side of the river. Dozens of submerged moss-covered stones and huge wet slimy boulders were hampering our progress. We carefully picked our way along the wet shingle of the riverbank through sliding, clacking pebbles, reaching out with our grazed fingers to the large boulders that were close at hand. The ground all around us was wet and slippery, which wasn't helping us in the slightest.

Minutes later, Isobel cautiously skipped across an exceptionally long line of stepping stones to the other side of the fast flowing river whilst I looked on, checking out which stones she stepped on, as I didn't want to slip and fall, ending up in the freezing, rushing water.

Satisfied she was safely on the other side, I nervously crossed over ... tripped on a submerged stone, twisting my ankle in the process, and ended up with my head and body submerged in the freezing frothy, raging water ...

In an instant, I found myself spinning amid a roaring swirl of swiftly-moving water. I instinctively snatched a lungful of precious air before I once again went under the ice-cold water, the strong force of the current dragging me further down to the bottom of the river. I began to panic as I was slowly running out of air. The next few seconds were a mad scramble as I tried with what little strength I had to reach the surface. Flailing amidst a sea of bubbles I fought for my life, at the same time trying to gain my bearings. The dark waters were making me disorientated, and I no longer had a sense of which way was up or down. Thankfully I caught sight of a faint shimmering light above me. So with a final determined effort, I pushed myself off the pebbled floor with my aching legs and swam towards it, coughing and gasping for air as I finally burst through the surface of the water.

I began to panic once again, still holding on to the stale breath in my burning lungs, at the same time treading water with my aching legs. Then, to my sheer joy, I caught sight of a log floating about four feet to the right of me. I quickly began to tread water with an exerted effort, pushing myself towards the log, my legs thumping and banging heavily against a hidden boulder in the river. I then found myself floating on my back, gasping for breath. But before I knew it, freezing cold water rode up and over my head once again, pummelling my face and chest. I suddenly sank like a stone to the bottom. My feet slipped and skidded under me on the slippy riverbed, and the top of my throbbing head thudded hard against something solid. It was the log I'd spotted a few terrifying seconds ago. I fumbled for a firmer footing, scattering a multitude of pebbles with my shoes in the process, reaching out for the log. I desperately grappled with the rough bark and the small leafy branches that sprouted from it. Gripping hold of the log for dear life with my now frozen fingers, the log slowly drifted towards the side of the riverbank, and safety. By some miracle I'd survived the terrifying ordeal.

Taking a deep breath, and shivering uncontrollably with the cold, I eventually managed to drag myself out of the river, bruised and winded, pulling myself upwards with sheer determination before collapsing face down on the wet shingle. My chest began to heave in spasms as I greedily sucked in great lungfuls of cold air and my tired muscles trembled.

Once my breathing was regular I glanced down, only to notice that my dirty hands were all covered in cuts and grazes, adding to my earlier wound. Small rivulets of blood slowly flowed between my dirty fingers, dripping into the cold river that had nearly taken me away. Then, kneeling down, I began to cough and retch up the foul dirty water from my lungs and throat. My head swam, blackness closed over my vision for several seconds and I buckled over onto my stomach.

I've no idea how long I was flaked out, shivering by the side of the stream, but it was the sound of Isobel's heavy breathing and intrepid footfalls that eventually brought me out of my daze.

"Oh, Barnaby. I thought you were going to drown. Are you all right? You haven't broken any bones, have you?" she asked, trembling with fear, brushing away the strands of wet hair from my forehead.

"I'm fine, thanks. I may have twisted my ankle when I first fell in. Just give me a few minutes will you so I can clear my head?" I sat there shivering from both the cold wind and my soaking wet clothes.

Then, to my amazement, Isobel slipped her jacket off, wrapping it around my trembling body. I glanced up into her concerned-looking eyes and smiled. She slowly crouched down and planted a kiss on my damp cheek, tears rolling down her dirt-smudged face, before settling down beside me, shivering. I opened the jacket a tad, slipping the edge of it around her shoulders with my arm. After a second she pressed as far under the jacket as she could towards me, trapping whatever body heat there was.

I hadn't a clue how long we were huddled together by the side of the river, I just knew I had completely misjudged Isobel. She was in actual fact a caring and loving person.

"Let's move away from here now, Barnaby. You can't afford to be sitting around in those wet clothes for too long. You need to be moving around to keep yourself warm. Here, stand up, so I can rub some warmth into your arms and legs."

Tears welled up in my eyes from Isobel's kind words, and I wasn't going to object. Anyway, at that moment I couldn't even feel my arms and legs, and my body ached all over.

Once I was certain I wasn't going to collapse in a heap on the floor, and I had enough feeling in my cold shivering body, I rolled over and pushed myself to my feet, though my body groaned in protest.

As we started to move away from the river, I looked down, focusing on taking one careful step at a time, picking my way carefully along the shingle of the riverbank towards a forest a few yards away. I draped my right arm over her shoulder whilst Isobel supported my weight by putting her left arm around my waist. Once again I was dizzy and unsteady on my feet, so I walked cautiously, one foot in front of the other. I ached everywhere. Not from sore muscles, but from simple exhaustion. And my wounded hand felt like it had been doused in petrol and set on fire.

The path to the woods was easy to follow, which was some small consolation. It took us through and by the gentle tree-lined hills and picturesque meadows of heather and gorse bushes. The wind sighed through the trees, sending dozens of leaves spinning down, adding to the thick, crunchy carpeting under our feet. We continued along the trail which took us past sweet-smelling pines. By this time my clothes were beginning to dry out, thank goodness.

"Let's stick to the path, it will be much safer," whispered Isobel. By now I was too tired to argue, so with my head bent down I carried on in silence, once again concentrating where I was putting my feet.

We'd only walked a short distance when we saw on the horizon fork lightning crashing to the ground, quickly followed by a vicious clap of thunder. Within seconds the rains came down in force. In an instant we were soaked to the skin. I thought I couldn't get any wetter, but I was totally wrong ...

"I'm sorry reader but I must rest awhile. I haven't slept for hours, and I need to get some well-earned sleep. You may be interested to know that so far I've written most of my adventures using odd scraps of paper where I can find them. I haven't much left now, so I need to use it sparingly, and I am hoping I don't run out of before I eventually finish my unbelievable account..."

Chapter Sixteen

At the northern edge of the woods meadows gave way to dusty, boulder-strewn slopes and craggy cliffs. The terrain was becoming difficult now, and the way was steep and covered with loose stones. It felt remote, and the only sound was the breeze. Thankfully, the rains had finally passed by, for the time being at least, and the welcoming rays from the morning sun were slowly drying my clothes out, which lifted my spirits, slightly.

Together we stepped between the fingers of rock which formed a winding pathway up the side of the hill. Several times we lost our footing and fell, but the unnerving sounds far off in the distance drove us quickly back to our feet, as we had no idea where the noise was coming from, or from whom?

After several tiring minutes of navigating the maze-like passageways that dotted the cliffs, we finally arrived at a wide ravine. We walked up to the edge of it, tentatively peering over the side of the vertiginous drop. Far below us were thick clouds combined with a fine water vapour, thrown up from the numerous waterfalls circling the ravine and spilling into a sheer precipice. The problem was that what we were witnessing was certainly not of this world, I was now pretty sure of that! Once again I had no intentions of raising the issue with Isobel. Anyway, if she had any common sense, she was now probably thinking the same as me.

"Well, Isobel, it seems the only safe passage across the

ravine is by that rickety old rope bridge over there," I said, pointing my shaky finger into the fine watery mist.

"We've no other choice, Barnaby. I'm up for it, are you?" she asked, nodding her head.

I anxiously nodded back. I was too exhausted to argue with her, and I was also eager to move on. I indicated for Isobel to start making her way to the bridge.

Falling into step beside her we cautiously, and somewhat stealthily, stepped out onto the bridge, clutching the frayed dangling wet rope on both sides for some means of support as it was swaying alarmingly with our clumsy movements. After taking a deep breath, and trying hard to control our nerves, we began to cross, one careful step at a time. We had just passed the halfway point when I thought I'd spotted something dark and menacing clambering up the far side of the ravine. It moved so quickly, I couldn't make out what it was. I decided not to say anything to Isobel as I didn't want to frighten her.

As we advanced toward the end the bridge it began to creak and judder with each heavy footstep. At that stage we paused awhile, trying our hardest to stop the rickety bridge from swaying like an out-of-control swing. Some five minutes later we had safely made it to the end, with us both letting out a big sigh of relief.

"I hope we don't come across anymore of those, Barnaby. I hate heights."

I broke out into a smile, "Now you tell me!"

Still shaken by our recent ordeal we began to cautiously head towards the bleak, cold moors, hoping to find the campsite and, more importantly, Aticuss and Fay.

Turning in the bend of the road, there was a lightning-bright flash in the sky overhead. I instinctively covered my eyes with my hands. When I removed them a few seconds later, I saw a small single-story building just a few yards away, and from this distance it seemed as though the building was deserted. There was no evidence of any kind of lights in any of the windows or farm vehicles parked in the driveway. It looked like an old deserted farm with a rambling collection of outbuildings sprawling down the hillside.

I grabbed hold of Isobel's cold, clammy hand for courage and we descended toward the ramshackle building, noticing a flock of crows circling over the nearby fields. Below them a fine grey mist hung like a shroud over the landscape.

At first the ground was uneven and boggy, so we found our progress becoming difficult and frustrating. It was a good job we didn't bring our bikes.

As we hastened through the broken gate to the farm, and across the deserted yard, I noticed that the back door of the farmhouse was hanging from one hinge, plus I spotted that most of the glass in the few windows was missing.

Hesitantly we approached the dilapidated building, nosily glancing over at the other farm buildings for any sign of life. All of them seemed eerily quiet, as if the place had been abandoned for years. Most of the shutters on the windows of the main building were missing, and the surrounding gardens showed clear signs of neglect. Odd shaped broken farm implements had been left to rust where they'd been dropped in the long grass, along with an assortment of wooden crates that had rotting food spilling out of the sides. Luckily for us we had our backs to the gusty wind, so we couldn't smell the decay that was no doubt seeping out from the crates.

Stretching up on my tiptoes, craning my neck, I sneakily peered in through one of the windows; noticing that the floor seemed to be clear of rubble, and most importantly it looked dry – thank goodness for small mercies, I thought.

Keeping as quite as possible we stealthily stepped through the unobstructed entrance finding ourselves in a square room made of wicker walls and peeling plaster, all caked with thick brown mud. High above us sunlight dappled through a crude thatch roof made of twigs and reeds, and beams of light caught the dust moats that gracefully floated through them. We both stood to survey the room, our eyes slowly adjusting to the sudden darkness. The inside was horrible and dusty. The floor was completely blanketed with bird droppings, mixed with broken glass and plaster, and it smelled. We should be getting used to that by now, don't you think?

Suddenly the wind began to whistle through the gaps in the windows, and what little glass was left in the frames rattled like a machine gun.

In the centre of the room was a rusty iron stove that squatted on short, bowed legs, and against the back wall a wooden bunk bed had collapsed in a heap onto the dirt-encrusted floor. There was also clear evidence that someone had started a small fire in one corner of the room. Regrettably there was nothing left to burn. Anyway, it wouldn't have made any difference. I had no matches on me.

I then slipped off my dripping jacket and ruffled my damp hair with my grazed and bloodied hands. At least the rain wasn't pouring through the roof – yet.

"What do you think has happened to Figment and Knuckledown, Barnaby?" whimpered Isobel as she surveyed the room.

I was far too busy drying myself at the time to answer

her. After a few minutes of jumping up and down on the spot I turned toward her, looking into her sad watery eyes.

"I wouldn't be too worried about them. Knowing Figment, he will find some way of not being caught. And after that magical encounter with the red mist and portal, I would assume he is safe and sound. We'll bump into him again soon enough, just you wait and see." Deep down I wasn't all that confident. But I didn't want to spook her, as I had a bad feeling in my gut.

I then began to roam around the room, windmilling my arms, trying to get myself warm. Luckily, it was working.

Meanwhile, Isobel had crossed the room to the open door, peering into the darkness.

In a flash she ducked down and crept toward me. She had her fingers pressed up to her mouth, indicating for me to be silent, at the same time jerking her head over to the right, just by one of the broken windows. It was then that I spotted what she was on about. Something dark and menacing passed by the open window. Sweat chilled my skin and I began to shiver, and that wasn't from my damp clothes. I searched the floor close by for some kind of weapon, but once again there was nothing I could use. "Damn!" My stomach shrank to the size of a pea.

"Isobel, what is it?" I whispered, crossing the room toward the stove on my tiptoes. By now my skin had erupted in goose bumps and the blood had drained from my face.

"I've no idea. I don't think we are alone" she whispered, her voice full of panic.

We both become silent, straining to listen for any kind of movement outside.

"There's someone out there," I whimpered, the hairs on the back of my neck beginning to prickle.

"I know there is, just be quiet will you?" muttered Isobel, under her breath.

We both scrambled for cover behind the stove for safety. Then all of a sudden a low hissing sound could be heard from somewhere outside in the dark. There is no mistaking that there was someone or something lurking out there in the dark. My heart almost missed a beat, and terror swept across both our faces.

"Keep your head down," I suggested, trying not to sneeze because of the dust we'd disturbed in our haste to hide. I could feel the *thud-thud-thud* of my heart in my chest. I tensed up, expecting the worse.

Outside I could hear footsteps on the gravel combined with a wet scraping noise. First it came somewhere off to my right, then in an instant it came from my left. "Maybe there is more than one person lurking around in the dark," I thought. That awful thought sent a chill down my spine once more.

Isobel moved a little closer to me as we both crouched down, rooted to the spot like two frozen statues. We held our breath, hoping that whoever was lurking just inches from us may not spot us huddled together inside. "No chance of that," I thought.

Just inches from the entrance the steps suddenly stopped. I squinted into the darkness, trying to determine where the visitor would appear, to the left or to the right of us? Then I heard something move outside. I tried to cry out and warn Isobel, but nothing came out – I was petrified and shaking with fear. The awful thought of what could be creeping out there sent butterflies fluttering in a frenzy around my stomach. I let out a breath I'd been holding for a long time.

Without any kind of warning the light dimmed a little as a ghostly figure filled the doorway, black against the rectangle of light. We both gave a start, and Isobel screamed. My heart was in my mouth. But before I could move there was a crash and a deep rumble that shook the foundations of the building, then the floor beneath our feet. Debris and twigs rained down from the ceiling. Within seconds the vibrations had stopped as quickly as they'd started. Then suddenly the building began to collapse around us. The walls crashed to the ground, churning up dust and shards of glass in the process. Then the wind blew hard like a tornado through the holes in the crumbing walls and open windows. The incredible force knocked us both onto our stomachs on the dirt-encrusted floor. The inside of the room resembled a dust storm I'd seen recently on the TV. Thick, choking dust spiralled all over the room, which made it difficult for us to see the entrance. Just then we both buried our dirt-spattered faces deep inside our coats to stop ourselves from choking.

And above the deafening noise of the wind I could hear laughter followed by a deep voice, rejoicing. Gradually the wind and falling debris from the building died down.

I don't know what came over me, but in a flash, I quickly picked myself up from the floor and grabbed Isobel by the arm. With our combined force we somehow managed to bulldoze our way through what was left of the doorway, surprising whoever it was, leaving the shadowy figure sprawled out on the dirt-covered ground.

"Don't look back, and keep your head down. I'm just hoping it's too disorientated to notice which way we're heading," I called out into Isobel's ear, helping her along the road.

As usual, I was totally wrong. Within a matter of seconds lightning bolts, too numerous to count, rained down around us, sending up plumes of smoke and dirt into the air, causing us to stumble and fall in a heap in a muddy bog.

Shaken and dazed I sprung to my feet and turned around, only to see to my alarm the ghostly shadow raising its arms, unleashing more lightning bolts from its fingertips. The blasts shook the ground beneath our feet. They were so close, I could smell the aroma of burnt grass, dirt and more worryingly, singed hair.

"You okay, Isobel?" I asked, struggling to catch my breath.

Isobel chewed her lip in silence for a while, startled. Eventually she answered.

"Yeah, thanks," she sighed, "I'm fine."

"Isobel, run like the wind and keep your head down. I don't think it's trying to hit us, she's only frightening us so we'll stop," I cried out above the noise going on around us. Sweat ran down my back, making my shirt stick to my already wet skin.

"Barnaby, *I am* frightened. It isn't everyday you take a stroll on the moors, only to be shot at," shouted Isobel, "And don't just stand there gawping like the village idiot. Help me up." After lifting her out of the mud, we sprinted towards a cluster of tall trees over to our left.

Isobel looked afraid. She was probably in shock, her mind reeling from what had just happened. I wasn't surprised!

For some unexplained reason the bolts had suddenly stopped, but yet to my horror I could still hear the sounds of unnerving squishy footfalls directly behind us.

I had no intentions of stopping to look back, so with

Isobel leading the way we crouched down and bounced along the springy heather towards the safety of the trees. We ran deeper into the woods. Low-hanging branches whipped my face and thick brambles snagged at my weary legs.

Nearing the thick copse of trees I could just make out a large cliff directly behind. At that stage I hoped we could reach the cliff before we were caught. There's bound to be somewhere in there we can hide. I certainly hoped so. Breath rasped hastily in my throat as I drove myself harder towards what I hoped was a safe refuge.

After a while I felt we had covered a good distance, but given we had been zigzagging for the past ten minutes we'd lost our sense of direction. So there was a slim chance we may be only a few metres from the farm building. Anyway it felt safe deep inside the forest with the trees pressing tightly on either side. Rain had soaked into the forest, thickening the mist that hung in patches. By this time sweat was pouring off me from the humidity.

Under the hazy sunlight, shining through the branches overhead, Isobel slowed down to a trot. Our heavy breathing echoed like a giant wall of sound. Thankfully, for the time being, no one seemed to be chasing us, so we stopped to get our breath back.

Over the next hour or so the weather worsened. It rained almost constantly, harder than before, soaking our clothes and leaving us cold and miserable. Yet we continued our journey with our heads down, following a well-trodden path into the woods, charging through low branches and brambles that smacked and stung our wet cheeks, snagging our clothes. Shafts of light flashed by as we raced along. The wind whipped through my hair.

The trees passed by in a blur as I constantly brushed away invisible strands of spider webs that clung to my face. I stopped to look up into the darkness beneath the trees, feeling a little uneasy.

"What if we were walking into some sort of trap?" I thought.

We made slow but steady progress through the woods. If the weather had been finer we'd have raced through, but the rain had led to mudslides and slippery underfoot conditions. We had to walk carefully, and we were often forced to backtrack and skirt around an area made inaccessible by the rain and thick squelching mud.

"Does it normally rain this much on the moors?" Isobel asked, mopping the rain from her face with her damp handkerchief.

"I haven't a clue, I've only visited the moors during the summer holidays," I replied, pulling my collar up to stop the rain from dripping down my neck.

After a short while the path quickly turned back into a much denser forest. At least we didn't have to worry at the moment about being seen by Nanny Whatcher-ma-call-it.

When we eventually left the forest it became more difficult, as we were now in the open on a bleak slope of a hill. The light increased the risk that we would be spotted, so we crouched down as low as possible, walking with utmost care.

We'd only moved a short distance when I heard a piercing cry cutting through the morning air. I could also hear something huge crashing through bushes and brambles just feet away. I slid to a halt, glancing back over my shoulder into the mist. Slowly emerging out of the swirling fog was what I could only describe as an old-fashioned 'clown'.

"What's happening to me?" I tried to clear my head, wondering if my frightening encounter in the freezing water had muddled my already mixed-up brain. But I just stood there, transfixed, staring, my mouth hung open. Things were all of a sudden starting to feel wrong ...

You're not going to believe this, but striding towards me was a circus clown. Yes, you heard me correctly; a circus clown was out here on the wild and windy moors. It had long funny tufts of ginger hair sprouting out on either side of its bald head, and there was a big gruesome clown smile painted over its mouth. It wore a big, baggy, silk chequered suit with huge red buttons, a bright yellow tie that flopped down the front of its shirt, and on its hands were big white gloves like the ones Mickey Mouse wore. It held a bunch of balloons of all colours like gorgeous ripe fruit on a stick and coming out of the mouth of the clown was a wheezy dry cackle which made my skin crawl. Its hideous cheesy smile chilled me to the bone. I never did like clowns, even when I saw them on the television in black and white. And then to come face-to-face with one in Technicolor made it even worse for me. I shuddered from the horrible sight.

"Barnaby, come on. Why have you stopped? We need to get away from here now," came the voice of Isobel. Unfortunately, I was still floating around in a dream-like state.

"The clown, can't you see the clown coming our way?" I cried out, stunned. Beads of sweat stood out on my forehead and I was struggling to breathe. My vision began to blur once again.

"We've somehow become trapped inside the faerie realm which Figment described to me. I'm sure of it," I called out, staring at the clown with unbridled fear.

"Barnaby, Nanny Buttonhole is playing tricks with your mind. There's no sign of a clown out there. It's just an awesome looking shadowy figure heading our way. And getting flipping closer with every step, so move your butt before we get caught," shouted Isobel in my ear.

Isobel must have been concerned about my state of mind because she slapped me hard across my cold cheek. Thankfully the shock brought me out of my waking nightmare.

"Here quickly, let me hold your hand, that way you will be able to see what I'm witnessing." I cried out above the noise.

In a flash I grabbed hold of her hand and turned her round to face the horrible clown emerging through the swirling mist.

"Barnaby! Oh, oh, I can see the clown now, sorry for doubting you."

Rubbing my now stinging cheek I gazed into the mist only to see the hideous colourful figure coming closer and closer with every long stride.

It was a tense, scary time as we were both at risk of being attacked at any moment by that *thing* heading our way.

We hastily ran away, cautious backwards steps at first, before turning tail, running for our lives, staggering through the mist towards the base of the cliff, our breath coming out in ragged breaths.

Once again, Isobel led the way, speeding across the heather, ducking through the undergrowth and along the overgrown path. I quickly followed, glancing over my shoulder to see if the shadowy figure had followed us. There was no sign of anyone, only the fine mist floating above the grass and heather. The sun then slowly disappeared from view behind the thick rain clouds and soon the forest was filled with lengthening eerie shadows. The cold wind gusted, forcing the branches to groan and creak around us. By now I felt both tired and hungry. But I knew there was no likelihood of stopping for a rest.

We then sluggishly slowed down to a trot, walking in silence for a while. My heart was racing with both fear and excitement. Once again I rubbed the nagging pain on the back of my hand. I blinked sweat out of my eyes, and the small trickle of blood from the back of my hand pattered down to the muddy ground.

Making our way along the path the heavens opened once more and a deluge began, the rain falling in hard from the west. Isobel's hair hung down like wet rats' tails, and I'm pretty sure I looked as bad.

We soon slowed down because the slope of the hill was steep and slippery with the rain and we kept on losing our balance. At one particular frightening point we almost fell into a heap at the bottom of the hill.

Suddenly we stopped mid-stride because the whole area was suddenly filled with the sound of wing beats, and then the sky became an inky blackness, blocking out what little sun there was. Then to our alarm a multitude of crows of all different sizes circled the dark sky, their cawing echoing across the wild and windy moors. I spotted thousands more perched on every available tree and rocky ledge of the cliffs. There were far too many to count, yet there was one particular large crow that had settled on a branch just feet from where we were standing. We cautiously walked over to investigate, hoping we wouldn't scare it away.

The crow shook itself; bits of feather drifted down before it beat its wings a few times. It then ruffled its feathers, proudly raising its head, cawing into the sky. The deep squawking echoed off the cliffs and travelled far off into the distance.

Then to our surprise, it stopped raining, suddenly followed by sleet, and then a heavy snowfall. Flakes the size of cornflakes came tumbling out of the sky. We both stood with our faces upturned to the fast-falling flakes which combined with the black speckled shadows flying all around us. Within seconds the moors were blanketed in snow.

Snow hushes everything but footfalls. I closed my eyes and strained to listen. There was no wind, no movement and no sound ...

Satisfied the coast was clear we slowly made our way toward the base of the snow-covered cliffs, scrambling over fallen branches that cracked noisily under our feet. We were making far too much noise to hope to evade the clown for my liking, so we decided to rest awhile, slumping down heavily on a small boulder, winded and spent.

Now that the shadow, or clown, was nowhere to be seen, for the time being at least, we decided it was time to climb the cliff.

To our astonishment, the thousands of birds around us never moved from their position. They just sat there motionless, staring at us, following our every movement, watching over us.

Above us the mountain rose up like the spine of a dark beast. We made little progress to begin with, slowly plodding onwards and upwards. As we climbed higher and higher, the going got harder and harder, stumbling along over ice-covered rocks. The wind was sharp up here, and we were soon chilled to the bone. The climb was steep and the grass was wet and coarse. The large tussocks of grass were dangerous and treacherous and the ground was uneven. It was getting darker as we got higher, and it would be easy to slip and twist an ankle.

Pausing to catch our breath we scanned the landscape behind us, seeing nothing, seeking something, someone hiding. We saw nothing but eyes watching ...

Minutes later we stopped and settled ourselves in a small hollow in the rocks. It gave us some small amount of protection from the cold biting wind. And then, without any kind of warning, the thousands of birds who'd been watching over our ascent for the past thirty minutes or so, took flight, fluttering noisily into the dreary sky, followed by a chorus of caws that echoed menacingly all over the moors. And in the distance a big storm was brewing, and the first rumbles had given way to crashes of thunder overhead and flashes of sheet lightning.

"Here it comes again," I said out loud as we edged our way beneath the overhang of the boulder for some shelter from the driving rain that was sure to follow.

"Hi there, reader. I hope you're not too frightened, and you don't decide not to finish my story. But you must understand, it's very important I tell someone about my eerie adventures before another innocent, trusting individual becomes trapped ... 'adventures', now that is a laugh when you consider what I've had to go through. It's more like a waking nightmare ... Sshh; I thought I heard the shuffling of feet and the sounds of grunting just feet from the door to my room. I do hope I don't have to move again. To tell you the truth, I'm totally exhausted, and I would love to curl up in a ball and fall fast asleep and not wake up. Just wait on a

minute, will you? I'm going to have to get up and check it out ...

... Nothing, thank goodness, there's no one out there this time. It was only the wind playing with the sides of this ramshackle building. You may have noticed that I'm becoming much braver. How long that will last, I've got no idea.

"Something's now screeching and yelling somewhere out there in the distance. I'm now wide-awake in total darkness wondering what the heck is going on out there. I've been in this position for so long I'm sort of used to it by now. But it's not getting any easier, I can assure you.

Chapter Seventeen

I woke up in agony with a thumping headache. The slightest movement sent sharp splinters of pain through my head and body, and my throat felt raw. Probably from the dry retching yesterday, I presumed. "But was yesterday an awful dream?" I thought, running my fingers through my damp hair. I instantly knew it wasn't when I spotted Isobel sitting down just a few feet from me, peering into the distance – she was looking for someone or something.

It was a pleasant morning. The sun was starting to take the chill from the air, and there wasn't even a cloud in the sky. Before us the sunlight illuminated the open land between where we stood and the edge of the forest. We were in a picturesque spot and the nearby trees didn't obscure our view. It looked so magical, and I wished we could sit here under pleasanter circumstances.

"Ah, you're finally awake ... lazy bones. Come on, shift yourself, it's about time we moved away from here," chuckled Isobel, pulling her jacket from my damp, aching body. She must have covered me during the night; how thoughtful of her.

In agony I struggled to my feet, brushing away the leaves and twigs from the seat of my pants, grimacing from the stab of pins and needles in my legs and arms. Glancing up into a clear blue sky I saw the sun, thankfully, was giving off a warm glow all over my damp body which made me shiver with pleasure for once.

"What do you think was in the caves with us the other night Isobel, and where on this Earth did all those crows come from? There must have been thousands of them," I said, stretching myself, trying to loosen my taught muscles.

"I've got no idea about the birds, and I'm certainly not going back into the cave to find out who or what's in there, that's for sure. Are you? And as far as that awesome clown is concerned, well I definitely don't want to bump into that thing again."

"I'd completely forgotten about the clown. I thought it was just a dream. And I've definitely no intentions of going back into the caves, but when you sit down and think about it, we actually didn't see anything out of the ordinary in the caves. It may have been our imagination. Also, we were both frightened and in a state of shock from the inky darkness ... Oh, by the way, thanks for the use of your jacket. You must have been cold during the night?" I said, struggling to find the right words.

"I was fine, and don't worry. I snuggled up to you halfway through the night to trap whatever body heat we had," she replied, turning her face from me. "Also, you may be interested to know that whilst you were snoring away, keeping me awake most of the night may I add, at no point did the sun drop below the horizon. It was dusk throughout the course of the long, lonely night. Also, the landscape and the trees look somehow different; magical, out of this world."

I agreed wholeheartedly with her, as I had already come to that conclusion hours ago. I was just surprised that she hadn't spotted it before now. Maybe because she was more concerned about my welfare? Then it suddenly struck me; those crows, could one of them have been Rustle, and was he watching over us?

"Barnaby, I know this is going to sound stupid, but I thought we were supposed to be searching for Aticuss and Fay, and not this Nanny Thing-a-ma-jig person. The way I see it, Thingy always seems to be hot on our tail. It looks to me as though it's guiding us to somewhere sinister, herding us like sheep. Don't you think that's weird?" she asked, raising her eyebrows.

A slight shiver crawled up my spine, even though I wasn't cold, and all of a sudden my legs felt wobbly, causing me to lean over into Isobel for support. By now I could barely see the ground at my feet, and it took me a while to clear my head.

"Are you okay, Barnaby?" she asked, concern in her voice.

"Yes, fine thanks," I lied. "I must have just gotten up too quickly, that's all. You know what it's like, don't you?"

"Yes, but you seem to be dizzy more than anyone else I know. Are you sure you're not on some kind of medication and you've forgotten all about it?"

"No," I replied, "so don't worry yourself, and I'm sure I'll be fine in a minute." Slyly and cautiously I began to caress the back of my throbbing hand. The wound was now slightly raised, as though a cat had scratched me, and the redness glowed beneath my skin. Also, alarmingly, I noticed that it had now spread right up to the knuckles. It was becoming painful to the touch and I had to grit my teeth from the smarting!

Well, you don't have to be a rocket scientist to realise that the thorn worming its way down into the back of my hand was a beacon for Nanny to follow, and Isobel had figured it out as well.

"Anyway, I can't see how she would know where to

find us. Mind you, having said that, she is some kind of nasty magical being," I said. As I already knew the answer, there was no point in arguing with her. What I needed to do was to get rid of the thorn right away. But how was I going to do that? Cut off my hand?

For a few minutes we sat in silence, staring at the sun slowly rising in the east, the cool breeze playing with Isobel's wispy hair ...

"Come on Isobel, we won't find Aticuss and Fay sat here. Which direction do you think we need to head in?" I asked, lifting my weary body off the floor.

"I've just been thinking. And I don't want any wisecracks coming from you," laughed Isobel, playfully thumping my arm. "Do you think when we stepped through that red portal in the cave that we somehow ended up in Fairyland? As I've said before, the landscape around here doesn't look the same as it did before we entered the cave. Do you agree?"

I felt now was the right time for me to explain to her what Figment had mentioned to me in my front room, about Fairyland always being dusky.

"You are totally correct, young lady. When I first met Figment and the others in my front room on Christmas morning he told me all about the magical world of Fairyland, how it never gets dark and the sky is always dusky. And when you think of it, the landscape does look unfamiliar, and the clouds seem much thicker and higher in the sky. Also, I've been in this part of the moors dozens of times with Mum and Dad for picnics, yet I don't remember there being so many forests and rushing streams around here, and especially those weird and wonderful waterfalls we came across," I said, shielding my eyes from the sun, scanning the scene before me.

145

"I hope one day, when we eventually get out of this mess, Figment will tell me all you know, it sounds really fascinating ..." she replied.

I then cut her off with a wave of my hand as I'd spotted something unusual in the distance.

"Sorry to interrupt you, Isobel, but is that a castle over there on the horizon? It looks from here to be made out of glass. That's weird. Can you see it as well?" I asked, pointing into the distance.

"Barnaby, I'm not too happy about all of this. And don't you be damn stupid and suggest we nip over there to investigate, because I am not moving an inch from this place until we find some answers elsewhere. Where from I've no idea, but I'm sure whoever's skulking around in that castle isn't going to be friendly. It never is in the fairy stories I've read."

Luckily, it didn't take me too long to convince Isobel that the only way we were going to get any kind of answers to the pickle we were in was to go and ask for help from the people who lived in the castle.

At first we started to trot, trying to keep ourselves warm, the two of us jogging side by side. And surprisingly we were both in good spirits, especially taking into account all that had just happened to us.

After about ten minutes we suddenly came across a wide area of deep, spongy moss and thick heather, which caused us to lose our footing a number of times. Because of this we stopped to rest a few times on the way. Also, the cold blustery wind sweeping across the open moors didn't help matters. It was getting darker due to the cloud cover gradually drifting over the sun and a thick bank of fog loomed in the distance, blocking out the top of the castle. Yet I knew it wouldn't get too dark to see where we were going, as I was pretty certain we *were* now in The Land of Fairies.

Finally we reached the fringes of the imposing-looking castle, which was blanketed in a fine mist. It had been built right on the edge of a rocky outcrop where it overhung the valley below. We also noticed the castle was connected by a narrow wooden bridge that was suspended over a drop of at least a hundred feet. When we'd first approached the castle we hadn't noticed that the cloud cover had virtually obscured the bridge; now we noticed that the castle wasn't made of glass after all. It was the inch-thick wet slimy lichen and glowing green algae that was glued to the stonewalls which the sun had been reflecting off.

The castle was set in its own grounds, and it was the most impressive castle I'd seen. Wide iron gates gave access to a wider gravel path that lead straight up the steps to a wooden front door. And from where we were stood the building looked to be very old and in a shocking state of repair. There were no signs of life from any of the windows. Yet I could imagine the leaded glass in the windows being so thick with grime and dirt, there was no chance of any light seeping through into the many rooms.

The light around us was now beginning to fail. The building itself seemed to radiate pure white light, yet it had a brooding presence. It felt enchanted. How I came to that conclusion was beyond me. It just felt that way at that time.

Then, without any kind of warning, a loud screech drew my attention skywards. Black shapes of every size suddenly appeared overhead, their spindly, feathered bodies silhouetted against the backdrop. Then another bird-like screech tore through the air and, before I knew it, there were literally dozens of answering calls all around us, echoing far into the distance. Had the birds come to watch over us once again?

"Just at that moment the heavens decided to open and within seconds we were both soaked to the skin. You've probably noticed over the past few hours that my clothes and hair have been more wet than dry."

Without any kind of warning, I quickly grabbed hold of Isobel's hand and dashed towards and over the wobbly wooden bridge, not thinking of the consequences; we could easily have slipped and fallen into the dark depths of the ravine.

"Barnaby let go of my hand this minute. There's no way I'm going over another bridge," she screamed, at the same time frantically trying to pull away from my grasp.

It was only when we stopped struggling with one another and arguing that we both realised we'd already walked half way across the bridge. We then took a deep breath before tentatively stepping into the cloud cover that was cloaking us, ending up by the start of a long gravel drive which lead up to the main door of the castle.

"Barnaby, you stupid idiot, we could have fallen off that tottering old bridge. Don't you ever listen to what I say?" she screamed at the top of her voice. Her whole body was shaking with anger.

"Well, young lady, if there's someone wandering around inside this place, they will definitely know they have visitors now. And stop being such a wimp, will you? The bridge was fine and dandy, and it seems when the owners built the bridge they had the foresight to string some thick netting across just feet below it as a precaution. I didn't spot it at first. Anyway, we need to take cover from this deluge, as we can't be hanging around any longer in these wet clothes. Come on, let's see if we can find a way inside."

"Going in by the front door is always the best bet," said Isobel, with lots of sarcasm in her voice.

"Good thinking, Batman, it's what I had in mind all along. Come on." I replied, glancing over my shoulder at a grinning Isobel. I smiled back and then headed in the direction of the castle.

We began to quicken our pace, squinting through the worsening rain. It was now coming down like stair rods, and the lightning made the clouds dance with shadow and flame, illuminating the building and our immediate area.

On reaching the top of the creaking stairs, we ended up facing a large elaborately carved double doorway made of black wood. We paused awhile to catch our breath, searching for some signs of life from the windows close by – nothing. The whole place seemed to be deserted. By now, the rain was pelting down in force, so I lifted my hand to knock. To our surprise, the door swung open of its own accord with a loud creaking of rusty hinges. Well, if there is anyone inside, they will certainly know they have guests from the amount of noise the door's made, in addition to Isobel's ranting and raving.

I smiled before opening my mouth, "Nice digs, the electricity bills must be enormous."

"Barnaby, we haven't got time to be messing around, and I don't think it's a good idea of yours to go snooping round someone's creepy old castle. Let's get out of here right away, I'm frightened," said Isobel, her voice hardly more than a whisper. The problem was, I was soaking wet and also eager to get out of the pouring rain. With that in mind I hastily stepped over the threshold into an inky darkness, reluctantly followed by Isobel. She didn't look very happy with me. Then the door shut again of its own accord! I looked back at the door in shock, but made no comment.

Once our eyes had become adjusted to the gloomy surroundings, we found ourselves in a large reception room, elegantly decorated with rich tapestries and fine oak-panelled walls. A number of faded portraits lined one of the walls and suits of armour decorated another. A long sturdy-looking table, large enough to seat some forty or fifty people stood in the centre, edged with huge wooden carved chairs. Feeling somewhat jaded I plonked myself down in one of the chairs, surveying the room. In the meantime, Isobel had crossed over to the other side of the large room, checking out the various doors for any sign of life. As for little old me, I was interested in the two wide staircases that spiralled upwards to either end of a balcony that overlooked the magnificent room. "Wow!"

I was just in the process of lifting my aching body from the chair to investigate the massive room when my ears caught the sound of another door being opened. Someone was in the castle, and coming our way!

"Did you hear that?" I whispered over to Isobel, "I think we've overstayed our welcome, so let's get the hell out of here."

Isobel didn't need to be told twice, and within seconds we were making a hasty retreat to the door.

Suddenly, from out of the corner of my eye, a shadowless figure appeared by my shoulder, its face just inches from mine. The rancid smell coming from its open mouth made me want to gag. Somehow I managed to hold down the bile that was forcing itself up my throat. How did it sneak up on us? I never heard a blooming thing.

"We meet once again, Mr Tinker-Tailor and friend. Welcome to my humble abode. Oh, I'm so sorry; I haven't introduced myself properly, have I? I'm Nanny Buttoncap and believe me, your worst nightmare. But not to worry, once I have you both listed in my little black book, all will be fine, I can assure you," she cackled loudly in my ear.

"How come you know my name?" I asked with some venom, trying to sound brave under the frightening circumstances I found myself in.

"Haven't you figured it out yet, young man? ... No. Shall I put you out of your misery? Go on then, I'll tell you; I like playing little games, don't you? What do you think is crawling around in the back of your hand, eh? That thing worming its way in your clammy skin is my way of keeping tabs on you, watching your every move which would eventually lead you to me." Once again she raised her face and laughed out loud, forcing the pictures on the walls to shake and the suits of armour to rattle and shuffle around on their stands as though there was someone alive and kicking inside, trying to force their way out.

"It's you. You're the nosey old man at the fair who wanted to see the Tree-Spirits, and then gave me this monstrosity that's been digging its way in the back of my hand for the past few days." I screamed, shoving my swollen hand into its upturned face. A shiver ran through my whole body from the pent-up anger I'd been holding back.

"Got it in one, young man," she laughed, her unblinking eyes burning into my brain.

Eventually her laughing came to an end, leaving her booming voice to slowly fade around the great room.

Without any kind of warning, Nanny quickly grabbed

me around the waist in a bear hug, before gripping tightly my throbbing hand. She then hovered one of her fingers just inches over the swollen wound. Ever so slowly, and painfully, I could feel the thorn embedded deep down in my skin worming its way to the surface. Sweat poured down my face like a river, stinging my already moist eyes. My whole body began to shake uncontrollably. It felt as though someone was sticking red-hot needles into my hand. I clenched my teeth hard from the searing pain.

Then my eyes began to lose their focus. I shook my head to clear it a little, as I tried in vain to pull away from her tight grasp. The pain encircling my whole body was excruciating, yet it was the thought of having the thorn removed from my injured hand that made me hold my nerve for a while longer. I just hoped and prayed the pain didn't last too long.

Suddenly my legs and body felt weak, like rubber. I then staggered a few paces like a drunken old man, crashing into Isobel, knocking us both heavily to the floor. Then in a blink of an eye, my world became just a black blur ...

"I'm sorry reader, but I need to take a short break to gather my thoughts. It's not easy you know, trying to recall everything that's happened to me over the past ... Sorry, but I can't remember how long it has been.

"Sometimes the memories come flooding back, yet there are other times when I have to quietly sit down and concentrate. The good news is that I no longer have the nightmares. How long that will last is anyone's guess.

"Most nights I lie awake for hours, tossing and turning, my eyes open, ears attuned to the sounds of silence around me. Every so often I lift my head when I

hear a distant noise, the rustle of the leaves on the trees, or the creaking of the old timbers of the ramshackle farm building I've found myself in. Each night passes with less sleep than the night before. I'm growing weaker by the day, and exhausted to the point of delirium. I now have trouble eating, even when I find food that's edible to eat ...

"Hey, just look at what I've found hidden in one of the dark corners of the room. It's a small cupboard, and guess what? It's filled from top to bottom with an assortment of tinned goods. It will be just my blooming luck that there won't be a tin opener anywhere... Found one ... Yippee!

"Now let's get this party started ... I'll be back shortly ...

Chapter Eighteen

I hadn't a clue how long I was unconscious; all I could remember was the horrible sensation like when you are going under when having a tooth out at the dentist.

"Barnaby, are you awake?" came the soothing voice of Isobel.

My eyes slowly began to focus, peering up into Isobel's watery eyes. "Here, take a sip of water, also don't move just yet, you took a nasty knock when you collapsed onto the stone floor."

Slowly I lifted my head, placing my chapped lips up against the small goblet she was holding to my mouth. The cold water felt like nectar as it trickled down my parched throat. A few drops spilled out of the corners of my mouth, dripping onto my jacket.

Once I was confident that I could move without fainting or retching I tentatively levered myself up on one elbow, surveying my strange surroundings. The room seemed to be some kind of cell. It was very small, no more than ten paces by four, with a heap of dirty straw in the corner that served as a bed. The walls were built from huge blocks of stone, all smooth and even, and then to my horror, there was no evidence of a door.

"Here Barnaby, let me help you sit up, and you'd be best using the wall to support yourself when you decide to stand, and I'm no spring chicken," laughed Isobel, attempting to lift me by my arms from the dusty floor.

"I suppose you've noticed that there isn't any sign of a

door anywhere," I said, rubbing the cramps from my legs and arms and then spotting my bloodied handkerchief, which was tightly wrapped around my stinging hand. Then I suddenly remembered the pain and agony of the thorn slowly sliding out of the back of my hand. I shuddered at the thought of it, but it was nice to know that the thorn wasn't inflicting any more damage.

"Yes, I've already spotted that. And don't ask me how we got into the room in the first place, because I was also out for the count. When you fainted you knocked me to the ground. I struck my head on the floor, and I only came too just a few minutes before you. And I've lump on the back of my head the size of an egg, thank you very much."

"Sorry about that," I replied, smiling, then lifting myself from the dusty floor. "Come on Isobel, we can't afford to wait until that monstrosity returns. Let's search in between the bricks and on the floor for some kind of lever. There must be a secret entrance situated somewhere in here. We can't have just been plonked in here through this stone wall or squeezed in between the metal bars. Hey, just hold on a minute, I've got a fantastic idea. I could huff and puff and blow the walls down," I added with a laugh. Isobel rolled her eyes, shook her head, and began to search the cell for some means of escape.

Fifteen minutes later we were still combing the crumbling stone walls and dusty floor for some means of getting out of this smelly cell. It was then that I felt we were going to be in here for a while longer, probably until Twelfth Night. "Let's hope they water and feed us before then?" I thought, despairingly.

We both decided it was a complete waste of time scrabbling around on the dusty floor, so we rested a while, leaning our weary bodies up against the wall.

As I was brushing away the grit and rubble from the seat of my pants my fingers brushed up against a small lever that was jutting out a few inches from the base of the wall.

Steadying myself by placing both feet against the wall, and with some trepidation, I pulled the lever. There was a couple of seconds of eerie silence before the sounds of grating and rumbling could be heard deep on the other side of the wall. It was the grinding sound of stone on stone. Then, within a matter of a few seconds, a small proportion of the wall began to crumble, revealing a narrow opening of a few inches. We stared at one another other, nodded, and jumped to our feet, climbing through the opening, not knowing what to expect on the other side.

To our surprise we found ourselves in a long, narrow passageway lit by hundreds of torches that were held in rusty iron conches at ten metre intervals. The soft radiant light reflecting off the walls was more than adequate to allow us to see our way down the passage. As our eyes gradually adjusted we began to see movement all around our feet, and on the walls.

Peering into the distance of the gloomy passageway we'd ended up in, we spotted dozens of large ugly spiders of every shape and size. They crawled up and down the chiselled walls before quickly disappearing into the cracks and crevices as they sensed our approach. Rats the size of new-born kittens were scurrying along the floor ahead of us, and droplets of water dripped from the roof into small pools with an eerie plopping sound that echoed around us. The air down here was cold, moist and dank. It also smelled as though something had crawled down here and died! Not again!

I can't actually recall how long we were scampering

down the long passageway because we were concentrating so much on where we were putting our feet. You see, the floor was awash with dozens of filthy rats and hundreds of gruesome spiders.

After going round in circles for what seemed like hours we suddenly came face to face with a solid brick wall. We'd come to a dead-end! Fortunately, there'd been sufficient light in the passageway to see the wall before either of us ran into it.

"That was close," I gasped, bending at the waist, trying to get my breath back. I was totally exhausted. I swallowed, forcing down a sudden feeling of childlike panic that started to bubble down in my belly and which threatened to come oozing up out of my throat. I was frightened.

"Can we rest awhile please, Barnaby? I'm shattered," wheezed Isobel. I could only nod my head in reply.

Rats moved stealthily in the shadows, and the floor was filled with small pools of water and piles of rubble. I then wondered if we'd missed a passageway as we were racing away from the cell. Somehow it didn't feel safe going back and searching for another way out, so after we'd got our breath back we carried on, our heads bent down, both feeling downhearted. "The point of no return?" I thought, with a heavy heart.

We followed the narrow passageway for another twenty minutes or so through dark tunnels, sometimes only a few feet high, and ended up in a rectangular chamber. The walls were coated in thick forests of glowing fungi, their pale light illuminating hundreds of giant glittering spider webs that hung down from the ceiling. Within each recess of the wall piles of broken bones and skulls were scattered on the floor, glinting in a ghostly glow around the room.

As we stepped further into the room we noticed three decaying skeletons, leaning against one of the walls. The stench in the chamber was eye-watering to say the least.

"I don't like the look of this, do you? Let's see if we fall lucky again. Start searching the walls for any signs of a loose brick out of place. There must be another secret entrance around here, or a panel somewhere, or a trigger of some kind. We should be getting used to this by now, don't you think? And DON'T disturb anything, especially the skeletons," I said, wrinkling my nose from the stench.

"You're a fun guy, Barnaby," giggled Isobel, clicking her tongue to wind me up.

I shook my head, laughing. "Don't blame me, you're the one who wanted a piece of the action."

I started groping blindly with my grazed fingers across the wall at one end while Isobel started on the opposite end.

After ten tense minutes we began to panic, accepting the fact we may have to retrace our steps back to the cell. But I wasn't going to give up that easily, not just yet anyway, so I frantically ran my hands all over the crumbling brickwork, searching for something out of the ordinary.

I was just beginning to think we were wasting our time when my fingers found a tiny groove in the wall. When I pressed against it a small, flat section of stone clicked and retracted. A switch must have triggered some kind of release, because that section of wall pivoted in the centre, turning outward, forming a door. Ever so slowly, the door scraped and dragged itself across the dust-coated floor. Dust rained down like snow, covering most of our hair. I started to laugh, pointing at Isobel's hair. It looked as though she'd become prematurely grey.

"Hah," I said with some satisfaction, "There we go, found it."

"Be careful, Barnaby, I can't imagine all secret passageways being safe; at least one of them must be hiding something nasty," Isobel whispered, panicking.

"Don't worry, I will, and don't you worry your little head." I replied sarcastically, which I regretted as soon as it left my mouth. "Sorry."

"You will be when you walk through the door and the floor suddenly opens up, with you ending up falling into a pit of venomous snakes and bubbling boiling water," she laughed, easing the tension between us.

"Well, they certainly knew how to build castles all those year ago. This one seems to be enormous," I called back over my shoulder to Isobel.

Isobel pressed forward, trying to step through the door, but I put a hand on her shoulder and stopped her.

"Just hang on. Let me go first. You never know what could be lurking on the other side," I whispered, sweat beading on my brow.

Isobel lifted her eyebrows and nodded.

I took a deep breath and passed through the doorway, into the darkness beyond. I narrowed my eyes, finding myself in a tunnel where the walls seemed to be made of loose earth and long, twisting tree roots. Thankfully, there was no nasty Shadow Thief about, so I called over my shoulder for Isobel to join me.

We then continued in silence for a while, our trainers kicking up clouds of dust as we scampered through the tunnel. Everything felt silent and cold. The only sound was the echo of our footsteps. We'd got no further than a few feet into the passageway when the ground beneath our feet suddenly began to vibrate, followed by the walls and the roof, showering us with chips of stone and dirt. At that point the floor gave way, with the two of us plummeting into darkness, yelling wildly as we fell. When I'd realised we were hurtling down a narrow tunnel, my first instincts were to lie flat on my back. It was a short, fast, frightening ride, the tunnel dropping sharply for many feet and then gradually levelling out. I came to a sudden stop several seconds later at the end, winded, and stretched out a foot, searching for the floor in the dark. I hadn't found it when Isobel barrelled into the back of me, sending me sprawling into open space. I opened my mouth to scream, but I hit the ground before I could. Luckily for us, the mouth of the tunnel was only a foot or two off the floor.

I haven't a clue how long we were sprawled out on the floor, it was just nice to know we were both alive. Well, I certainly was, because I could feel the aches and pains down my spine and on my backside. I could also see Isobel brushing away the dust from her hands and hair. And to my surprise, she was laughing away to herself.

"That was fun. Can we do that again, Barnaby? I haven't had so much fun in my life."

I couldn't help it, I started to giggle. "Once is enough, thanks very much. We don't want to spoil you, now do we?" I laughed out loud.

Once we were certain we hadn't broken any bones, and we were only slightly shaken by our ordeal, we decided to sit down for a while to recover our breath. It also took us a while to stop giggling, but it did ease the tension between us, thankfully.

After a ten-minute rest we decided to carry on, traipsing down the long winding tunnel, noticing that our surroundings were gradually changing. The ceiling was becoming higher, and I could see a number of dead leaves and dust devils spinning across the dirt-covered floor. That could mean only one thing. There must be a draft coming from somewhere in the tunnel. I could have sat down and cried.

"You may be interested to know, I think we may have found a way out of here. Look, there seems to be a draft coming from somewhere over in that direction," I said, ruffling my hair, ridding it of the grey dust.

Isobel sauntered over and gave me a big cuddle. "I'm frightened Barnaby," she cried, her sobs bouncing off the walls.

It isn't every day I have a young lady using my shoulder as a handkerchief, but I did feel some responsibility for her being here. With that in mind, I began to soothe her by gently rubbing her back; at the same time trying to reassure her that everything would work out just fine ... I hoped.

"I may not show it outwardly," I said, "But I'm petrified. What we are going through normally happens to kids in fairy stories. Also, if I'd not gone to the fair in the first place, none of this would be happening. Let's not dwell on that at the moment; let's go and see if we can find where this draft is coming from. No doubt there will be another secret passage somewhere or a hidden lever we have to find before we can get out, as nothing seems to be simple for us, does it?"

"Okay, and let's not be too downhearted, Barnaby. With our combined brainpower we've managed to get this far. Come on, let's get our jeans dirty once more and start looking for this draft, you never know, this time we may find a door to the outside world." It was nice to see her spirits had lifted.

I wasn't quite as optimistic as Isobel but I did as I was told, dropping down on all fours, sweeping away the dust with my hands across the floor, trying to locate where the draft was coming from.

"Barnaby, come over here quickly. I've found a tunnel that has been covered with tree roots and vines. You never know, it may lead us up to the surface. And I can also see a small chink of light. Can you see it? There's also a ladder running up the side of the tunnel." With that good piece of news, we both collapsed to the floor, embracing each other, rocking back and forth.

"I can tell you this, reader, that was one of the best feelings I've ever had in my young life!"

After an embarrassing few minutes of cuddling and giving each other words of comfort, we separated, preparing ourselves to climb to the top of the rickety ladder, all the while listening out to what may be waiting for us on the surface.

The rungs of the ladders creaked in protest under our combined weight, so we stopped now and again to make sure the ladders wasn't going to come away from its mountings.

Nearing the top of the tunnel I could hear the unnerving sounds of slow footsteps from where we'd come heading our way. It was then that Isobel pushed me from behind, urging me to move as quickly as possible up the ladder. I didn't need another shove from her, and I was soon making my way up like a crazed monkey.

Just feet from the top I hadn't noticed that one of the rungs was missing, and I slipped and lost my grip, dangling in mid-air by one hand, with my trainers just inches from

Isobel's head. Luckily, Isobel had spotted the pickle I was in and, with her help; I managed to pull myself back onto the ladder.

"Thanks."

"No problem, that's what friends are for."

Once again I tried to hold down a lump that was forming in my throat.

Without further incident, I managed to reach the top of the ladders. I then wedged my feet at both ends of the rungs to keep my balance before reaching out with my hands toward the top. Stretching up on my tiptoes, my hand surprisingly disappeared through the surface. It wasn't solid, as I'd expected, it was just clumps of grass and thick moist soil that was covering the opening.

"Thank goodness for small mercies," I whispered to myself.

Within minutes we were both safely on the surface, slumping down on the wet grass, taking in the beautiful landscape around us, breathing in the cool, clean air. It was wonderful. The sun burnt brightly in the clear blue sky above us, highlighting the vast moors and bare rocky hills. We just sat there and stared in silence ...

"Time for another break. Also, I think I've overstayed my welcome in this hovel, and I seriously need to start thinking of moving away soon. Don't worry; I'm always ready to leave at a moment's notice. No doubt you've realised I'm on the run from some gruesome and unfriendly neighbours.

"Just hold on there. I thought this place looked familiar when I first arrived. I must have stayed here some months ago. I can see the sweet wrappers and rusty tins of beans I'd piled up in the corner. That just

shows you. I've no idea what's happening to me.

"Will it ever end, I wonder? Because, at this moment in time, I don't know how long I can carry on like this ..."

Chapter Nineteen

"Penny for them," said the wispy voice, directly behind my left shoulder.

"Penny for what?" I replied, rubbing my eyes.

"Your thoughts, silly boy," came the reply.

"Oh! I was just wondering where Figment and the rest of the team had got to, that's all," I sighed, taking in the breath-taking scenery before me.

"Much nearer than you think, I guess, Barnaby," answered the voice just inches from my right ear.

Planting my hands firmly on the grassy ground, I quickly spun around, suddenly aware that Isobel was below and to the left of me. So who had spoken?

"Figment," I cried out in alarm.

The big robed figure stepped toward me and gave me a bear hug before lifting me up off the ground.

"Where on earth did you come from? I never heard your footsteps, you sly old thing. Did you just materialise out of thin air, or did you come through one of those fairy portals?" I asked, trying to get my breath and composure back.

"Barnaby, what's wrong with Figment's eyes? They look bugged and he's not blinking!" bellowed Isobel, grabbing me by the elbow and then dragging me unceremoniously down the hill.

"You're not Figment at all, you're Nanny Buttoncap. We've done you no harm, so why can't you leave us alone?" I yelled back over my shoulder.

Nanny murmured something in a strange tongue I couldn't make out, at the same time adding a roll of her wrist and a graceful ripple of her fingers.

I instantly felt her spell lock around me like a full-body straitjacket, paralysing me from chin to toes, wrapping me in a silent, unseen force. It pressed hard up against my clothes, flattening them, and it also made it hard for me to take a deep breath. I couldn't move an inch. Then the skin on the back of my neck tried to crawl up over my head and hide in my mouth. I was terrified.

Moving gracefully toward me, Nanny stood almost close enough to touch me. "You have something I will never have, little boy – Figment's friendship and loyalty. Did he not tell you that I am his wicked sister, and the black sheep of the family? You are also my ticket to getting Figment finally into my clutches; how else do you think I could find him, you silly, silly boy?" she cackled, her face now inches from mine. From where I was, *she* also seemed to be hovering just inches from the ground.

So that's it. She'd been using me all along to capture Figment, waiting for him to appear and rescue us. And also messing about with my head! How stupid of me; if I'd only just stopped for a few minutes to work the whole thing out. Anyway, what could I do now? Nothing, really. Also, Nanny is Figment's sibling. I wonder why he never mentioned it to me. Oh dear, I do hope he appears soon. We need his help like crazy ...

I stood there, paralysed, feeling the fabric of the spell closing all around me. But I did have the satisfaction of seeing Isobel sneakily edging her way down the hill. Then my joy turned to horror, as Nanny flicked one of her fingers at Isobel. And in a blink of an eye, she too was in Nanny's spell.

With a cruel smile spread across her grisly face, Nanny slightly raised one of her fingers, twirling it around in the air before our terrified eyes. Instantly we began to float, higher and higher from the ground, while turning around to face the open vista that lay before us. I felt so helpless.

I couldn't believe my eyes. The whole hillside was lit up by thousands of brightly-coloured lights. Jewels twinkled from every blade of grass. Then in the next instant a fine mist rose inches from the ground forming a wave, followed by an unearthly image of white horses with quivering nostrils, broad chests and large white eyes. Every horse was shod with silver, their hooves striking the ground in a shower of white sparks, and seated majestically on top of each horse was a knight. Each knight had a jewel in its forehead in the shape of a star, and they wore green mantles finished off with gold. Golden helmets were fixed on their heads, and they held a golden spear. "These must be 'The Unseelie Court'?" I thought, despairingly. My heart pounded with terror, and I shook like a leaf before the magical scene materialising before me.

Then, out of the undulating mist, hundreds of living, breathing, stinking creatures of every imaginable shape and size materialised before my eyes, all-howling with blood-lust fury. The vast majority of them were ugly and grotesque in shape. I couldn't help but notice a few of them grunting and groaning as their bodies became inflated into some gruesome monstrosity. Others reminded me of the dwarves in Snow White, yet I don't think the ones in front of me were as good-natured as those. Making up the numbers were a variety of pixies and wood elves which I'd recently seen in a school textbook. The wood elves seemed to be completely covered in a tight one-piece skin-like material which looked to be wet and coloured like the bark of a tree. The whole ground seemed to be swarming with thousands of fireflies. A chill ran down my spine and I felt useless, looking at the army of hundreds of marauding creatures heading in my direction.

By this time I wasn't too bothered about the sight of the pixies as I was terrified. You're probably wondering how I can remember each and every one of them so clearly – well you see, as they were advancing towards me, I was slowly but surely getting closer to them by the second. The hordes of grotesque creatures then crowded around us, hemming us in. All of them were focused on yours truly.

By now my feet were firmly on the ground! Yet, I knew I was still under Nanny's spell, because when I attempted to move my hands toward the back pocket of my jeans for the four-leaf clovers, I couldn't move them. They were securely fixed by my sides!

"Friends of yours, Barnaby, and where's your manners? Aren't you going to introduce them to me?" giggled Isobel. "You seem to attract shadowy figures like bees to a honey jar," she added, letting out a pent-up breath.

I suddenly got the giggles. Don't ask me why, but under the circumstances, it seemed damned funny at the time. And, to be honest, it isn't every day you come across hundreds of gruesome and abnormal creatures, now is it?

"You should be honoured." I replied from out of the corner of my mouth, tears forming in my already moist eyes. Once again I started to lose my balance, and the illusion began to distort my vision. Was there before me an illusion? I couldn't be too sure. Yet Isobel was witnessing the whole thing ...

Chapter Twenty

"Oh, at last, you're finally awake. I'm so glad, as I didn't want you to miss the fun," said the voice from somewhere deep in the back of my head. I couldn't be sure if I was dreaming or if I was awake. Yet the voice said I was awake, so I must be.

Slowly but surely my heavy eyes began to open, only to see to my horror Nanny sat in an enormous winged chair next to an open blazing fire. And I couldn't be entirely certain, but I thought I heard the sounds of fluttering wings coming from somewhere in the shadows of the room. Being nosey, at the same time hoping to find a way out of this horrible predicament, I managed; with some effort may I add, to cautiously ease myself up from the uncomfortable bed I was lying on.

Once my eyes had become accustomed to the flickering glow of the fire, I spotted in the corner a large ornate antique-looking birdcage. And from this distance it looked as though it was built to keep large animals in. Then, I couldn't believe my eyes; Tickety-Boo and Rosie Apple were both locked up inside the cage and, to make matters worse, there was also the limp form of Figment laid out in one corner of the room, motionless. My whole body shuddered as I gazed helplessly at him. How did Nanny manage to capture Figment? Was it my entire fault, and had Figment come to my aid on the moors? Did he sense the danger I'd found myself in? There were far too many questions for me to answer at the moment. And there was one other worrying thing I had to consider. Where was my friend Isobel?

"What have you done with Isobel?" I screamed, searching out the dark corners of the room.

"Oh her, she's on the floor, by the side of the bed. There was only enough space on the bed for the one of you, and she was too heavy to lift," laughed Nanny at her silly joke. I wasn't laughing, I was concerned about Isobel.

I leapt out of bed and knelt down next to the prone body of Isobel. My new trusting and considerate friend!

"Isobel, can you hear me. It's Barnaby," I whispered in her ear, carefully supporting the back of her head with my hand whilst resting her limp body against my chest.

"Isobel. Please wake up," I implored, feeling downhearted and lost without her.

Then I remembered the four-leaf clovers tucked inside the back pocket of my jeans. I wondered if they would help. After sifting through the accumulation of rubbish I pulled out, there was no sign of the clovers.

"Looking for these?" asked Nanny, waving the four-leaf clovers around in her fingers.

"Shit."

"Now, now, young man, your parents wouldn't be very happy hearing that kind of language coming from someone as young as you, would they?"

"You'd make a vicar swear, and what have you done with Isobel? She won't wake up."

"Give her time. She's not as strong as you," she said smugly.

Just then Isobel began to stir, groaning and shuffling about, trying to fight her way from my grip.

"Isobel, it's me, Barnaby, and please don't struggle, you will only hurt yourself. Also, don't be too alarmed when you open your eyes. It seems Nanny has the awesome power to capture and hold the most powerful guardians."

"What are you going on about, Barnaby? ... Oh no, that's not Rosie Apple and Tickety-Boo locked up in that awful cage, is it? And who's that laid out on the floor in the corner? Please tell me it's not Figment, Barnaby!"

I didn't have the heart to tell her at that precise moment. So I began to stroke her hair, hoping to calm her down from the shock.

When Nanny lifted herself off the chair, I decided to pull Isobel to her feet, so at least we weren't both looking up into her hideous face. Once I felt sure we weren't going to fall in a heap on the floor, we made our way over to the lifeless figure of Figment.

"Stay where you are," ordered Nanny with a flick of her wrist. Her eyes were fixed on us both, green-blue like glacial ice, unblinking.

Once again we were rooted to the spot.

"What are you going to do with us?" I asked, at the same time twisting my head toward Isobel, checking to make sure she was fine. To my relief, she was.

"With us? Don't flatter yourself; it's him I want, not you two mere mortals who are no threat to me at all. I've spent years, no not years, centuries, searching for that on the floor. When I first met you at the fair, I knew you would fall into my trap. The problem I had was that I needed Figment to be in a safe house and come to life. Whilst he was in the form of a doll, along with his two annoying Spirits, I couldn't do anything. He had to be whole, living and breathing. I knew it was only a matter of time before he came to your aid. And then I had to find some way of getting you to the moors, as I knew he would watch over you. That's when the thorn came to my aid, as you already know. Once I have his powers, I will be invincible, and you wouldn't imagine in a trillion years the havoc I will unleash on this pathetic world of yours." Then she must have laughed for at least five minutes.

I just stood there, motionless, staring at the manic-looking women in front of me. I also had the added problem that I was still under her spell and I couldn't move a single inch. I thought I was going out of my mind.

Eventually she stopped laughing, before clicking her fingers down toward Figment, who in turn woke up in a start. I noticed a rippling effect circling his whole body, as though he was blanketed in water. Must be one of Nanny's spells to keep Figment from escaping, I assumed.

"Well hello, big brother of mine. We meet once again, but this time under different circumstances. I'm in charge for a change, and yes, I've also got your winged buddies to keep you company, along with the two mortals you keep losing." Once again she began to laugh at her own joke. "And not forgetting the troublesome Tree-Spirits who are safely hidden away from nosey-parkers."

"You won't get away with this, Nanny, there are too many 'Good Folk' out there who will move Heaven and Earth to stop you from being immortal," shouted Figment from the shadows.

"Heaven and Earth you say Figment, you may be correct on that particular point. Let's not lose sight of the fact, it's this Earth I want, so if they need any help, I'm at their service, ha ha ha."

I didn't like the sound of any of that. And I had no idea what was to follow. I just hoped there was someone or something out there on the moors that may aid us in our hour of need. Who that was, I hadn't a clue. I was also intrigued to know where Nanny had imprisoned Aticuss and Fay.

Just when I thought it couldn't get any worse, one of the large wooden doors to our right opened up. A gruesome gap-toothed dwarf stepped through into the room with a few of his horrible friends tagging along behind. The dwarf's hands and feet were huge. They were all out of proportion to the rest of his body. He had thick legs like tree trunks, and his hairy ears turned upwards to a point. His nose was also pointed, and his mouth was wide, similar to the opening of a post box. He was BUTT UGLY! The rest of them weren't any better, and the smell coming from them made me want to gag.

Then I had a terrible feeling. In all of this mayhem and running about that's been going on, I'd completely forgotten about Mum and Dad. They must be beside themselves with worry.

All of a sudden, memories, images washed through me, dozens of little things I'd forgotten came back to me all at once: my mother's laugh, quiet and cheeky. And the comforting, warm feeling of her being next to me in bed when I'd woken up in the night from a nasty dream, and then finding her fast asleep on the pillow beside me, gentle and peaceful in the morning sun. There were many more memories, but I pushed them aside as I was now becoming tearful.

I then recalled Figment saying to me that time slowed down in the presence of faeries. I hoped he was right!

It was Nanny who broke my concentration as I held back the lump in my throat.

"Escort all three to the altar, the sun will be setting soon, and watch over them with your lives; also, don't forget the cage in the corner. I want those two to witness

174

the ceremony from a close distance," she cackled as she brushed passed the dwarf.

What on earth is going to happen to us out there, I wondered? It doesn't bear thinking about!

Moments later we were being escorted through the immense castle, passing dazzling suits of armour and beautiful ornate tapestries that stretched all the way to the ceiling. This place was far too good for the likes of someone like Nanny Buttoncap, I thought, despairingly.

In the meantime, Figment and Isobel had reached the main door to the castle. And from where I was standing I could hear the unnerving sounds of stomping feet and the clatter of metal against metal outside. Oh dear, those horrible creatures we'd bumped into before were waiting outside for us.

As soon as the main door opened a large assortment of dwarfs, hobgoblins and many more monstrosities began to cheer and shout. The loud screeching voices were a cacophony of sound that bounced back into the great hall.

My mouth fell open at the gruesome sight. But it was the unexpected shove in my back that brought me out of my waking nightmare. Then Nanny suddenly appeared close by, holding up the cage before her. Where were my two friends? Please don't tell me she'd killed them. I then heard quiet sobbing coming directly from the cage.

"What have you done to them?" I screamed with rage.

"Open your eyes, stupid boy. Can't you see; they're laid out on the floor of the cage? But don't concern yourself about those two, it's your fate you need to be worried about. Now move yourselves before I cast another nasty spell on you all," she cried, barging her way past the three of us.

With another sharp poke in my back from one of the creatures we were guided up a steep hill towards what looked like some kind of weird altar, decorated with all kinds of flowers and herbs. The air grew cold enough to sting my hands and face.

Some minutes later we came to a halt, suddenly becoming aware of our surroundings. The scene that lay before me was what I can only describe as magical.

I gritted my teeth and closed my eyes for a second, shuddering from the view.

Opening my eyes a crack, I began to stagger from the mysterious sight. In the far-off distance there were long rolling hills, all filled with vines of green and flowers of gold and silver that spilled out over the snowy hilltops like a translucent garden. Fields of red and blue brushed up against the dense forest. The light was so vibrant I couldn't look directly at it.

Directly in front of me was the beginning of a narrow path that stretched for miles; as far as the eyes could see. It wound and twisted its way towards a destination that I couldn't see. Glancing down at my feet I saw that the path was made from springy, velvety moss; the most luxurious and perfect moss that I'd ever come across. All of a sudden I felt brave, so I took one little step onto the path. As my feet touched the moss it lit up with a luminous emerald-green glow. The light illuminated my wet sneakers, bathing the mossy path in a luminescent shimmer for just a fleeting instant. I stood still for a few moments, simply looking down at the moss, noticing that it was peppered with starlight that sparkled and glittered back at me as if I was walking on magic itself. I took a few tentative steps along the path, moving with dreamlike slowness. With each step I took I could see the emerald light surrounding me, and with every footstep the glittering starlight bounced up and enveloped my whole body. At the same time I was being showered with a powder puff of glittering faerie dust. The further I walked upon the path, the more encompassed I became in shimmering green light and sparkles of sunlight. The light and dust had now risen so high that they danced like fireflies around my head. Then all at once I was surrounded in a brilliance of green light and stardust, which engulfed me so much that I couldn't see the pathway ahead. I took a few moments to take in the experience, watching closely the dancing spectacle of light and luminosity. I'd never in my short life seen anything as wondrous as this. It was then when I wondered whether Isobel was having the same experience as I was.

My joy quickly turned to sadness when I heard the bellowing coming from Nanny, bringing me out of my amazing dream world. Or was it, I pondered? I hoped not as it was too beautiful to describe fully.

Then, before my dreamy eyes, Nanny, to my sheer horror, produced a large leather-bound book from under her flowing cloak – 'The Book of Tormented Shadows' I guessed. I was definitely now becoming scared, and I could see Isobel was scared as well. When Nanny had her head buried in the book, I sidled over to Isobel, groping around blindly for her trembling hand.

From this distance it looked as though Nanny was setting herself up for something spectacular!

"You two. Have you any idea what this is?" Nanny shouted across to us, lifting up the book above her head with both hands for us to see.

I certainly did, but I didn't want to scare Isobel, so I shouted, "NO, but I'm damn sure you're going to tell us!" I called out through gritted teeth. I was now feeling brave.

"Impertinent boy. Because of your rudeness, I'll put your name in the book first, followed by your girlfriend."

"She's not my ..." I abruptly stopped what I was saying; aware Isobel was staring into my eyes. I smiled at her, and she returned the smile, gently squeezing my hand.

"Please don't list her name in the book, I beg you. I bought the Tree-Spirits and Figment. Please let her go, and I know you can from all the wise words I've heard over the last twenty-four hours, or just minutes in Fairyland ..."

Nanny raised her hand for silence, cutting me off. "How sweet you humans are. I'll think about it, in the meantime your name will appear on the top of a brand-new page. You should feel honoured," she informed me, before slamming the book shut with an almighty thud.

Without any kind of warning the winds howled from the trees, whipping into a savage circle of moving air, lifting up wet leaves, twigs and small stones. I then felt a sudden rush of wind stirring at my clothes and ruffling my damp hair, tearing at the misty ground like the downblast of a helicopter. All of a sudden a large black blob appeared in the sky, followed by hundreds more. Unexpectedly there was a flash of sheet lightning directly above us, and then out of the sky dropped more dark shapes, swooping low over our heads toward Nanny Buttoncap. Everything became dark and all around us thousands upon thousands of birds plunged and dived in between us. Some of the birds peeled off, diving towards Nanny, all screeching to each other, as if already celebrating a quick kill.

Yet, for some unknown reason, the other birds missed the three of us completely. They were only attacking the hundreds of creatures below us and, more importantly, Nanny Buttoncap, who by now was raising her hands to the skies, sending out bolts of lightning that struck dozens of birds as they circled and swept around her. Her dark eyes glowed in triumph.

From the fields below us came a deep rumbling sound. It began as a low moan, and within seconds it rose to a wail. Then it became a screaming mob, the sounds of roaring and howling, with blood-lust fury. The roar shattered my senses and made my heart and belly shiver with the sheer force of it. Everything around me was chaos and confusion.

"I need to finish my story as quickly as possible now, as I am finding concentrating difficult. My body is so weary and my eyes are becoming tired from all of this writing I've been doing. Let's hope I can manage to put down everything that's happened to me. As I said to you before, you need to be aware of my unearthly encounters before another unsuspecting mortal ... sorry, I don't have the courage to write down my thoughts at this moment in time as it is too distressing."

Chapter Twenty-One

Fear can literally feel like ice water. It can be a cold feeling that you swallow, that rolls down your throat and spreads into your whole body ... I swallowed a mouthful of fear, my eyes fixed on what was slowly emerging through the swirling grey mist.

Hundreds of creatures sprang into ranks, all armed with bows and arrows, spears and slings, which they used to take down as many birds as they could. The air was filled with hundreds of swooping black birds, adding to the hundreds of quivering arrows that rained down all around us.

Bolts of lightning cut through the sky from all angles as the clouds began to part, revealing an outraged Nanny in all her glory. She began to ripple and expand; huge, bulging muscles erupted all over her body like angry festering boils. It wasn't a pretty sight.

I took a deep breath and tried to get my heart rate under control.

Enormous coloured gouts of fire darted here and there from her fingertips, exploding on the ground in small, steaming puddles. Large deep holes materialised in the ground around our feet, scattering clumps of earth and burnt grass high into the air. Some of the stray bolts struck a number of trees close by; the trees splintered and fell to the ground into a shower of sparks and burning shreds of wood. One titanic blast ripped a six-foot trench in the earth just inches from the tips of my trainers. The choking, thick smoke smothered me, forcing me to cough and splutter. My vision blurred and my eyes began to sting.

All around me were the whispers of things moving in the smoke, combined with soft, hungry hisses and the gleam of malevolent red eyes. My heart pounded in my throat. I remained motionless for a moment, stunned, wiping my moist eyes with the back of my hand.

Peering through the thick swirling smoke at an angry Nanny, I noticed that the book had somehow slipped out of her hand onto the muddy ground by her feet. And to my joy, it looked as though she wasn't aware of it. Yet one particular large crow was, and within seconds it, and dozens of others, flew down and attacked the book with gusto, tearing the pages to shreds.

"Rustle." I cried above the noise. The crow cocked its head and looked across, and I'm pretty sure it also winked at me ...

Nanny was so wrapped up with what was going on around her the spell she had on Figment had disappeared – thank goodness! And also, to my sheer delight, I spotted the large gilded cage lying on its side in the thick mud with its door wide open. Had Tickety-Boo and Rosie Apple escaped from Nanny's clutches, I wondered? I certainly hoped so.

I then looked up in time to see Figment shake his head before sending out his own bolts of lightning at Nanny, who was now totally oblivious to his presence. One after another lances of crimson energy, white at their core, leapt out at the speed of light from his outstretched fingertips. One of the bolts exploded just inches from Nanny's feet, showering her with dirt and clods of burnt grass. Nanny hastily spun round to see where the lightning bolts had come from, realising to

181

her surprise it was Figment. Within seconds a curtain of blazing scarlet energy materialised in front of her, protecting her from the pulsating energy that was being launched at her. Then the ground beneath her feet began to boil and vibrate, forming a deep crater, with little frightened old me standing dead centre. Sprawled all around its edges were well over a dozen grotesque bodies, each burned beyond recognition, and to my sorrow, thousands of birds lay motionless on the dirt-encrusted ground by my muddy trainers. Floating left and right in the cold evening air were thousands of glowing burnt feathers, all landing majestically on the blood-stained ground, all combined with tiny shreds of paper from 'The Book of Tormented Shadows'. I quickly turned my back against the images of the nightmarish carnage around me, feeling upset and guilty for putting the birds and Isobel in so much danger ...

As the strips of paper touched the sodden ground, minute pinpricks of sparkling light materialised in the mist, similar to soap bubbles from a child's toy, followed by the appearance of an ethereal figure of a small child, then another, and then a multitude appeared out of the mist. In a blinding flash, hundreds of dazzling colourful streaks darted down from the sky, exploding into small particles as they touched the ground. Every one of them contained a tiny human at its centre; yet no shadows were evident from a single one of them. I was mesmerised by the breathtaking sight, spellbound. I could find no other words to describe it.

Gracefully, one after another, the figures alighted from their enchanted bubble, sending out puffs of glowing silver dust motes into the air. I've no doubt these were the many faeries and innocent children Nanny had listed in her book ... then I remembered the pouch.

"How on earth do we get it from Nanny?" I asked myself, slapping myself on the forehead. "I know. The crows," I shouted with joy, clicking my fingers.

I hastily looked around and found Isobel close at hand, staring back at me with wide eyes. "What did you say, Barnaby?" squealed Isobel as she ducked down from the many explosions going on all around us.

"I need to get word to Rustle, right away. He has to find some way of getting the pouch off Nanny, and then I need to release the shadows from the pouch."

"What the heck is a Rustle?" asked Isobel, raising her eyebrows.

"Follow me and I'll tell you," I shouted over the explosions.

I didn't bother answering at first because I was concentrating so much, scrambling on my hands and knees toward my black friend, Rustle. The cold rain made the ground slippery with mud, slowing my progress. I then began to give Isobel a shortened version of how I took care of Rustle, which she thought was big-hearted of me.

When we were just inches from the excited crows they suddenly stopped what they were doing, instead gazing across at me in wonder.

"You're a sight for sore eyes, and thanks for your help so far. Anyway, I don't know if you can understand me, but I need you to get hold of a brown leather pouch that's attached to the inside of Nanny's tunic. The pouch holds the shadows of the hundreds of faeries and humans she's stolen over the years ..." I stopped short, realising I must have looked ridiculous resting on my hands and knees, talking to a multitude of quizzical-looking birds.

Yet somehow though, they must have understood me, because in a matter of seconds, Rustle and a few of the others swooped down toward an unwary Nanny.

Within a matter of seconds, Nanny was completely buried in a tide of black feathers and sharp, snapping beaks. I also noticed somewhere deep in the fracas two small stunning faeries fighting with Nanny's torn and tattered cloak. It was Tickety-Boo and Rosie Apple. They *had* escaped from the cage. I would have wept if it wasn't for the fighting and explosions going on around me. Then suddenly, appearing from the almighty scrap, one particular large crow flew from the bunch, clutching a small brown bag in its beak ... THE POUCH.

"Yippee!" I shouted, jumping up and down on the spot. Then my joy turned to sadness as Nanny worked one of her spells on the birds that were blanketing her. Scorched black feathers and small bits of flesh and bone exploded in the air, followed by a deep guttural roar that made everyone on the moors stop and watch. It was Nanny, and she was becoming larger by the second... "Oh Shhh ... sugar!"

No one moved. I couldn't, because Rustle was lying by my feet – dead.

Pain hit me, sharp and low, just beneath my heart, as though someone had just shoved an icicle through me. Tears came to my eyes and I wept aloud, clutching my dear friend close to my chest.

Isobel knelt down beside me, wrapping her arm around my shoulder, giving me some words of comfort. But it wasn't working. I was beside myself with grief. A little bird had tried to help me; who would have believed it?

"Come on Barnaby, don't grieve for him, he was just returning a favour. If you hadn't nursed him back to health all those months ago, he couldn't have helped you, now could he?"

I knew she was right, again. We needed to find a way out of this nightmare. And where had Figment disappeared to?

Not to worry, like everyone else on the moors he was witnessing the gruesome figure of Nanny rising menacingly up into the night sky.

I waited for a moment, my breath steaming before me. I then carefully laid Rustle on the ground by a small bush, as I didn't want anyone to stand on him. After whispering my goodbyes, we made our way over to Figment, hoping he had a way of getting us out of this terrible mess. Yet from the frightening expression on his face, I wasn't holding out much hope.

Taking several stumbling steps, my feet struck something. I stopped to look down. It was the pouch. Bright, cold blue light washed over it in a wave, blinding me for a second. I cautiously picked the bag up in my sweaty fingers. Then the pouch began to stir in my trembling hands. My heart almost skipped a beat. Keeping as calm and composed as possible under the circumstances, I began to loosen the drawstring before peering down into the bag. It contained a thick mass of black shadows, all merging together as one. Yet the pouch felt light as a feather.

Out of the murky gloom came a wild screeching sound. I instinctively spun around, dropping the pouch on the muddy ground in the process.

Coming towards us like a steam train was a mass of gruesome bodies, all sweeping out of the rolling mist. They moved like crazed, out-of-control animals, closing in on all sides, surrounding us. Twisted, bulging faces and glowing red eyes stared menacingly back at us through the fog.

I frantically scanned the floor for the pouch, but it had vanished. I just hoped and prayed that the many shadows trapped inside would find a way out before Nanny became aware that it was missing from her person.

"How do we aim to get away from that?" I whispered over at Figment, pointing at the horrible sight of Nanny Buttoncap.

"Be patient." That's all he said.

He didn't sound too convincing for my liking, so I gripped Isobel's hand, manoeuvring our way through the dead birds and injured creatures towards the woods, hoping no one would spot what we were up to. Especially Nanny!

Battling our way through the clogging mud and lifeless creatures I bent down to collect a sword from a dead goblin; the weight giving me the feeling of power as I swept it left and right in front of me.

"And where do you think you're going?" came the booming voice of Nanny from a height of about twenty feet.

"Oh, oh, we'll have to go to Plan B, Isobel."

"What's Plan B?" she croaked.

"Plan B is ... run like the wind and don't stop to look back," I screamed above the clamour around us.

"You've got to be kidding me, Barnaby. From her vantage point she could destroy anything for miles around. Just stop will you, and let's think about our next move."

Fortunately, I didn't have to stop and listen to what Isobel had to say, because the hundreds of birds were now flying in formation, circling before us, forming an enormous long black tunnel. But more importantly, Nanny and her minions wouldn't be able to see where we were going, once we were safely inside.

Unfortunately, there was one slight problem we had to sort out first. A huge grotesque troll, at least ten feet tall, its skin upholstered in knobbly, hairy warts, lank hair hanging greasily past its massive shoulders, tiny red-veined eyes glaring from beneath its rugged brow deep within its head, was blocking our path. Its nostrils flared out, quivering. Thick drool dribbled from its fat lips. Its legs were firmly planted apart in an offensive stance. It was enormous, and hideous, and it didn't look happy for my liking. Its massive jaw hung open, with long thick strings of saliva dripping from out of the corners of its mouth. It hissed and howled. Its glowing red-veined eyes fixed on me with a glare that made me shudder with fright. In a flash it produced an awesome looking spear from behind its back before sprinting towards me at break-neck speed, screaming and shaking the spear in the air. Stodgy drool sprayed left and right from its mouth, landing with a hiss on the ground. Isobel screamed.

With the troll just inches from us, I stepped forward in a defensive stance, giddy with rage. I ducked down at the last second before sweeping the spear to one side with my sword, cutting the shaft of the spear in half. Undeterred, it came onto me again, teeth bared. I couldn't move an inch; my mouth hung open waiting for the inevitable. Then before I knew it, it swung its beefy hand towards my head. I quickly came to my senses and, in a flash, I stepped to my right and bobbed down. His beefy hand was just inches from the top of my head. I fell to the ground so hard that all the breath was driven out of my body, and in an instant the troll was bearing down on me once again. I quickly rolled over in the mud and blood a couple of times, hoping to confuse it. All around me, I heard the unnerving sounds of goblins and trolls, their growls bubbling up in their throats. I froze, my heart pounding in my ears, and my legs started shaking in naked fear. I knew that to survive the next few seconds, I had to find someway to get away from the angry, ugly troll.

Before I could think what to do, Figment shoved the creature to one side with a sweep of his hand. The creature fell hard to the ground, dead. Figment glanced across and nodded to me. I nodded back, wiping the sweat from my brow, at the same time ensuring the sword was firmly gripped in my trembling hand.

Despite being short and ungainly, the rest of the mixture of creatures surrounding us proved to be accomplished fighters, and it took all of Figment's skills and my pathetic swordsmanship to fend off their frenzied attacks. It wasn't easy you know, trying to cautiously step around the mutilated bodies on the ground, and keeping my balance at the same time. And more importantly, not getting myself killed in the process!

I had only a second's warning, the sound of wheezing and snarling coming up from behind me, when something large and furry slammed into my legs, just below my knees, taking them out from under me and sending me heavily to the muddy ground. Summoning all of my remaining strength I let out a piercing cry and swung my sword like a baseball bat in the air, feeling it crack down solidly on something hard and bony. There was a snarl, a deep animal sound, and then something tore the sword from my hand, sending it spinning away. The sword landed with a loud squelch in the mud. I quickly got my feet underneath me and back-pedalled, yelling out my fear into the night. I then stood still for a second, staring into the mist that was floating before me. I'd half expected the creature to return, but nothing happened. I couldn't hear anything. I held my breath, not daring to move, lest the motion gave me away.

"Had something or someone scared it off?" I thought, letting out the breath I was holding, thankful I was alive.

Chapter Twenty-Two

By now I was splattered with mud and blood and shivering out-of-control from the cold biting wind, realising that I could have been killed. But if I'm shivering, I know I must be alive. I lifted my face to the sky, wiping the rain from my hair, slicking it back.

Thunder growled near at hand. Lightning danced and flickered overhead, casting odd light and spectral shadows through the thick clouds. Another storm was brewing.

I've got no idea how long I was staring down at the dead creatures by my feet, the raindrops slapping on my head, but the next thing I remember was Isobel dragging me toward the tunnel the birds had formed. It looked never ending.

Aware we had an opportunity to escape we quickly sprinted toward the opening, running for our lives, all the time not knowing what to expect at the other end. I knew then we weren't going to get away that lightly. I kept my eyes moving left and right, my senses alert. By now Nanny was firing hundreds of lightning bolts at the birds that were protecting us. Scores of dead birds tumbled to the floor by our feet, their feathers singed, their tiny bodies in flames. Tears welled up in my eyes, and the noise of battle going on around us seemed to be hundreds of miles away.

I hadn't realised, but Figment was also making his way down the tunnel.

"Figment, how do we stop her? Can't you do anything?"

I wheezed, holding Isobel's hand, as I didn't want to lose her.

"We have to take her eyes out," he said, as though it wasn't a problem.

"WHAT!" I screamed. I tried to calm my pounding heart, focusing on where I was putting my feet.

"Yes, there's no other way, believe me, Barnaby."

"I do believe you, I do, but how do you intend doing that?" I asked, rubbing the stitch in my side.

"Knuckledown."

"Knuckledown? How on earth do you expect a plastercine figure to beat the might of Nanny? Poke her eyes out with his hands and legs?" I laughed nervously, shaking my head.

"Got it in one, Barnaby. Before Nanny put me under her dreaming spell, I sneakily slipped Knuckledown inside the folds of her hood. Let's just wait and see, shall we?"

"I couldn't believe my ears. Knuckledown is going to save the day ... my handmade decoration. It's just so unbelievable, don't you think? Go and kick her butt."

Well, there was no point in discussing it with him any further; I had to take Figment's word for it. And I couldn't even hazard a guess as to what Knuckledown was getting up to at this moment.

The tunnel went on and on for what seemed like miles. The hundreds of birds caused an almighty draft in front of us as we carried on towards, hopefully, safety. Some tiring ten minutes later I could see a small flicker of moonlight up ahead. By the time we reached the end of the tunnel we were all shattered, so we cautiously stepped through the exit, not knowing what to expect.

But as soon as we left the tunnel, the birds dispersed into the night sky. And over the vast open moors there were thousands of tiny pinpricks of light, sparkling and glowing in the dark. Suddenly, additional lights appeared in the mist that floated in the distance. Then, in a flash, the small lights exploded, revealing dark outlines, the size of small children. Amazingly, none of the forms had any evidence of a shadow. Then in an instant, hundreds of thousands of small, slithering inky-black forms floated across the moors toward the figures. I was so engrossed in the scene before me that I hadn't noticed the multitude of frightened creatures rushing past us, taking no notice of us, running into the darkness beyond.

"I wonder what spooked that lot?" I asked to no one in particular. By now our faces were streaked with sweat, dust and fear.

"Her," answered Figment, pointing at the wavering figure of Nanny Buttoncap on the horizon.

She must have stood twenty feet tall. Her fat face was warped; twisted and distorted. Suddenly, darkness enfolded her and she screamed, out-of-control, staggering about, reaching out blindly with her outstretched hands ... I then understood the reason why she was acting like this. She couldn't see where she was going. Knuckledown had somehow managed to blind her. How, I've no idea, but that wasn't important. What was crucial was that Figment might now be able to finish her off.

I turned to face Figment to ask him what he intended doing, only to see him marching toward the figure of Nanny, flexing his long lean fingers. I really didn't want to see what he had in store for her, so I stepped across to be beside Isobel, embracing her and then burying my head deep into her shoulder. I was glad I had my eyes shut because a powerful blue flare pierced my eyelids, resulting in small blue lights floating before my eyes.

Then the air cracked with thunder, rushing air whipped my clothes, and the hairs on the back of my neck stood up. A cold shudder glided up and down my spine. With a gurgling death cry from Nanny, the rest of the creatures gave out a cowardly whimper before turning tail, fleeing like fury to the nearby woods.

I then found the courage to see what was actually happening to Nanny.

They say the bigger they are, the harder they fall, and as far as Nanny was concerned, it certainly was in her case.

Slowly but surely she began to teeter backwards on her heels, arms flailing in the air, trying very hard to keep her balance, her back arched. Fear touched the corners of what was left of her eyes; she knew she was doomed.

Then, to my disgust, her rib cage expanded outwards through her skin. Bleached bones stuck out like ragged sharp knives, quickly followed by arterial blood that sprayed out of her body in all directions, showering the dozens of creatures racing past her, leaving a large gooey pool of sticky blood on the ground along with thick pulped, gelatinous masses of flesh that had to be what remained of her cruel heart.

Another guttural roar sliced through the night air before the ground shook as the mighty beast hit the ground with a powerful thud, throwing up thick clouds of mud, dirt and blood. Then, in a blinding blue flash, Nanny Buttoncap exploded in a cloud of dust before vanishing like a *presence* in the cold evening air.

Surprisingly the night turned into a summer's day, and I had to shield my eyes with my hand from the blazing sun. Then, flaming bits of something that I didn't want to think about rained down by our feet, landing with little, wet, plopping sounds, hissing into spluttering coolness. There was no way I could have recognised the remains for what they were. My stomach curled up on itself and I forced myself to look away.

Everywhere I looked there were dead birds and creatures, cloaking the ground, all blackened and charred, which caused me to shudder at the sight. Once again, tears streamed down my face, glancing across at the hundreds of birds who'd come to our aid. I was also trying my hardest to hold back the burning bile that rose up in my throat from witnessing the awful image of Nanny Buttoncap's demise.

Before I knew it, my stomach suddenly revolted and I collapsed on my knees in the red sludge, throwing up the contents of my stomach.

It was while I was breathing hard, trying to clear the bile from my mouth, that my concentration was abruptly interrupted.

Just a few feet from me, faerie folk of every shape and size mysteriously appeared before my eyes. They were all smiling, and they walked with grace. Starlight shimmered on their hair and in their piercing blue eyes. They bore no lights, yet as they walked, a shimmer, like the light of the moon seemed to fall about their feet as they silently passed by like shadows, without sound or footfall. Some of them were mounted on highly-strung pure-white horses which were shod with silver shoes and adorned with golden bridles. They had jingling bells in their manes which sang like angels singing. The horses left a beautiful trail of shimmering golden lights behind them as they trotted gracefully side-by-side, lighting up the hillside and giving off a magical glow. To my joy, two

194

of the fairy folk passing by were Aticuss and Fay. They both reined their majestic horses to a stop beside me and bowed their heads before following the rest of the folk into the mist. I stood there with my mouth gaping, feeling at ease for the first time in ages.

I've no idea how long I held Isobel in a tight embrace, mesmerised by the ethereal scene of the faeries disappearing before us, as it was an embarrassed cough that brought us out of our musing. It was Figment.

"There's nothing more we can do here. It's time for you both to go home. Come on," ordered Figment.

As we parted, I planted a kiss on Isobel's forehead and stepped across to Figment, as I wanted to know what had happened to Nanny. He didn't tell me, as he said it was too upsetting to relive the moment he returned his sister to the 'Middle Kingdom' for an eternity. I didn't press him any further as I could see he was grieving.

"Where did Knuckledown get to, is he back with you?" I asked.

It was at this point that Figment informed me that Knuckledown had unfortunately accompanied Nanny to 'The Kingdom', and he was so sorry to be the bearer of bad news.

"Well, at least he's alive, and knowing him, he will somehow make it as comfortable as possible. Take care old friend," I shouted, wiping a lonely tear from my cheek.

Little by little the hundreds of living, breathing, stinking creatures drew back down the hill. No more gruesome creatures wandered around looking for a fight. Within minutes the moors were completely empty of the enemy.

As we stood reflecting over what had just happened, the sun came out from behind the clouds, shining on the enchanting scene around us. In that flash of sunlight all was revealed, as I swept my eyes left and right across the moors. In the far distance, thousands of small bubbles of light, the colours of a rainbow, hovered over the ground before flickering off in a blink of an eye, leaving the moors in brilliant sunshine. I hadn't realised, but I was holding my breath. Luckily, it was Figment who brought me out of my musing once again.

"Prepare to be taken back to your own world. And as I said to you before, when in The Land of Faeries, time slows down; so don't worry about your parents. They won't be any wiser, trust me," said Figment with his usual reassuring smile. He then magically produced Tickety-Boo and Rosy Apple from under his cloak. To my joy, they didn't seem to have been harmed in any way.

"Don't concern yourselves with these two little ones, I'll look after them. And you never know, Barnaby, they may suddenly appear on your Christmas tree one year when you are least expecting it," he said, carefully placing them both in the pocket of his cloak.

Just then my concentration was broken when a small scattering of pages from 'The Book of Tormented Shadows' blew past my feet. I hastily bent down to pick a few of them up.

Spread across the yellowing pages was a spider-crawl of fading ink, written in lines that sloped and rose untidily, as though someone had written the words down in a hurry. At first I struggled to make any sense of the words. Then it hit me. These were the names of just some of the thousands of shadows Nanny had stolen over the centuries. But, to my horror, only one page was completely intact!

Time seemed to slow down, to almost a stop, and before I knew it, I was whisked away to somewhere I couldn't even begin to describe. Darkness swallowed me. There was nothing but silence where I drifted, nothing but endless night. No thoughts, no dreams, no nothing ...

"There won't be any point in you going out onto the wild and windy moors, searching for me, hoping to bump into me.

"Why you ask?

"I'll tell you why.

"After all the fighting and bloodshed had finally come to its grisly end, 'The Book' had only one page that was left completely intact. And, unfortunately for me, that page had my name clearly written on it. And now I'm trapped in this unforgiving, alien world forever ...

"But please don't concern yourself. You see, there comes a point in everyone's life when they have to take stock of things – I've had to over the years.

"Please don't look at me like that ... I've accepted the predicament I've now found myself in – so why can't you?

"Now the only thing I have left to keep me from going insane are the fond memories of my short childhood and my loving Mother and Father, not forgetting my new-found friend, Isobel. And as for Figment saying that I may see my two hand-made Christmas decorations one year ... If only.

"I do have the satisfaction of knowing that I had a hand in releasing those thousands upon thousands of trapped Tree-Spirits and unsuspecting mortals ...

"Yet I do still cling to the false hope that one day I may eventually escape, even though I know its madness. Because you see reader, I've been here far, far too long..."

"Hi ...

"I've been patiently waiting, wondering how long it would be before you came around to reading my book.

But what made you decide?

Was it the hairs on the back of your neck standing up when you first picked it up, or the tingle in your fingertips?

"Anyway, let's not concern ourselves with that at the moment, what counts is that you have taken the first step in my incredible and terrifying journey.

"But before you begin, I would strongly suggest that you make yourself comfortable, as you may not want to put the book down once you have started, and more importantly, when you do eventually decide to rest your eyes, please ensure you keep the book well hidden because you wouldn't want the wicked ...

"Sssh, don't say a word and just act normally. I have an awful feeling someone is watching us. Can you sense it as well . . ?

"It's fine; don't be alarmed or worried. It was only my imagination running riot as usual ... or was it . . ?

"I'm so sorry about that: I hope I didn't scare you, and more importantly, it hasn't put you off reading the rest of my story...

"Now, where was I . . ? Oh yes, I remember now.

"To tell you the truth, I've had a hard time of it lately, owing to the fact that I have to hastily move at short notice from one deserted hideout to another. I'm also finding it difficult concentrating due to the lack of sleep, and I've completely lost track of time. And to add to my misery, the freezing cold draught coming

198

in through the shattered window over to my right is making it extremely difficult for me to put the words down onto paper. I am just hoping and praying that someone can find the time and patience to translate my wobbly handwriting ...

"Sorry, how rude of me. I haven't introduced myself properly, have I?

"My name is Barnaby Tinker-Tailor, and I believe it's only right that I tell someone about my unearthly experiences that began on the evening of the 23rd December 1967. I was just twelve years old at the time, and if I'd known then what I know now, I most certainly would have done things a whole lot differently ..."